"Come, sit down." She patted the bed.

Liz sat with a shy smile. "I don't know about you, but that book drove me crazy."

"I can see why," Joan said, meeting Liz's eyes boldly, letting the lust show.

Liz slid a little closer. "Do you . . . would you . . . ?"

"Yes, I want to. Right now."

"Maybe I should . . ." Liz said, getting up.

"No." Joan grabbed her wrist, pulling her off balance so that Liz fell on the bed.

Somehow they became entwined in an awkward embrace. But the kissing that followed was neither clumsy nor shy . . .

Birds
of a
Feather

JACKIE CALHOUN

THE NAIAD PRESS, INC.
1999

Printed in the United States of America on acid-free paper
First Edition

Editor: Lila Empson
Cover designer: Bonnie Liss (Phoenix Graphics)
Typesetter: Sandi Stancil

Library of Congress Cataloging-in-Publication Data

Calhoun, Jackie.
    Birds of a feather / by Jackie Calhoun.
        p.   cm.
    ISBN 1-56280-240-2   (alk. paper)
    I. Title.
PS3553.A3985B57   1999
813'.54—dc21   98-46229
                                                                              CIP

To Diane,
who makes life enjoyable

ACKNOWLEDGMENT

I want to thank my good friend, Joan Hendry, for reading my manuscripts. I depend on her ready support, her honest criticism, and her editorial commentary and corrections.

ABOUT THE AUTHOR

Jackie Calhoun is the author of ten Naiad books and
has stories in five Naiad anthologies. She lives with
her partner in Wisconsin.

BOOKS BY JACKIE CALHOUN

Lifestyles

Second Chance

Sticks and Stones

Friends and Lovers

Triple Exposure

Changes

Love or Money

Seasons of the Heart

By Reservation Only

Birds of a Feather

Summer

I

Mist rose around Joan's feet as whatever cooling the night had offered dissipated in the rising sun. Shades of red splashed the eastern sky. She peered through her Bausch & Lomb binoculars at the yellow warbler in the sumac grove. Satisfied that she'd identified the bird, she watched it flit to another branch, then fly away.

The boardwalk creaked under her hiking boots. She often tromped through these wetlands on her daily walk. Hearing a high, thin scream, she looked up and spied a red-tailed hawk wheeling overhead. It dropped like a stone, its talons spread, toward some hapless creature, but she knew more often than not its prey escaped.

She'd have to leave soon if she were going to shower and grab a bite to eat before opening the Birds of a Feather store at nine.

Already the day was warm, windless, the air dense with humidity. Mosquitoes buzzed around her bare legs, but she ignored them for a moment to stand and listen to the birds loudly proclaiming their territories with song.

Winters were long in Wisconsin. To survive one made her more appreciative of the green seasons, as she called them. She loved this time of year and soaked up the warmth like her old dog, who lay panting at her feet.

"Come on, buddy, time to go."

The dog, a mix of yellow Lab and golden retriever looked up at her, his tail thumping on the boards, before struggling to his feet. He had the hip problems that come to large dogs with age, but he was always waiting at the door when it was time to leave. And she lacked the heart to tell him to stay.

Walking to her car, a battered blue Bronco she'd bought secondhand, she unlocked the driver's side and climbed in. Her binos she slid under the seat. They were the only valuable she left in the car. She gave the dog a boost onto the back seat.

"Up you go, boy. Time to go to work."

Unrolling the window partway, she climbed behind the wheel. Turning the key, she heard a click. She turned it again, unable to believe that on this hot morning her car refused to start. But she'd had fair warning that there were battery problems looming

4

Getting out, she lifted the hood and wiggled the battery cable posts. Then she opened the tailgate and took out the battery brush and a half-inch wrench. After cleaning the posts, she tightened the clamps and hopped back in the Bronco.

"Here we go, guy. Hang on."

The dog panted in her ear. His breath was enough to knock her out. You really had to love him, she thought, and she did. He was a great dog.

This time there was a puny whirring sound, and the engine suddenly caught. She felt enormous relief. No one else was parked in the lot. It was only seven A.M. Putting the vehicle in drive, she headed toward her small house, the one she put all her savings down on last fall.

She knew she had to have it when she walked into it the first time. Downstairs were the living room with fireplace, the dining area, the kitchen, and a bedroom and bath. An open area between the two bedrooms and half bath in the second floor loft overlooked the living room. She couldn't have designed a house better suited for her wants. The windows in the living room looked out at the country road that fronted the half-acre lot. The other windows faced the woods surrounding the yard. The twelve hundred square feet had made the house affordable.

Parking the Bronco in the driveway before the one-and-a-half-car garage, another reason the asking price was reasonable, she let the dog out. There was no one to wave at her as he picked up the Saturday newspaper. She lived on the edge of town, but all the lots around hers were for sale.

Knowing she had to hurry, she took her clothes off on the way to the shower. The water was barely hot before she turned it off and got out. Drying her graying hair, she opened the door to let the steam out of the room. Yeller lay stretched out on the wood floor.

She dressed in jeans and T-shirt and went into the kitchen where she toasted a couple of pieces of bread.

"I got to get out of here," she said to the dog, who was now lying in the middle of the kitchen floor. He was good company, following her around the house, banging his tail when she spoke to him.

The phone rang.

"Hey, girlfriend, someone's coming in for some of those bird ornaments. They're packed in the storeroom, but the box is labeled."

"It's summer," she said. "Why would anyone want ornaments?"

"Ask him. Maybe he shops early." Kathy owned the store along with her husband. "What are you doing home anyway?"

"I'm not. See you later." She grabbed her backpack and the toast. "Come on, buddy boy. Let's go."

The dog once more lurched to his feet and followed her to the Bronco. She helped him get into the vehicle and backed it out of the driveway. The store was thirty minutes away.

Unlocking the door, she switched on the lights and the music. They had tapes of different birdcalls, which Kathy wanted played in hopes that the customers would buy some of them.

It wasn't quite nine, so she relocked the door and went to the storeroom in search of the bird ornaments. Finding the box, she carried it to the checkout counter in the middle of the large room. Then she opened the store for business.

Not that there were hordes of people who came into the place Saturdays, but there were plenty to keep it open. Kathy worked the store the other five days of the week.

But Joan was getting a little burned out. Working six days a week to pay for a house made no sense. You never had time to enjoy the place. Weekdays she worked up front at a feed mill, essentially doing the same thing. They also sold birdseed and feeders.

And then what did she do mornings? Bird-watch. Was she crazy? she wondered, leaning on the counter and staring out the plate glass window. There was more to life than owning a house, caring for a dog, watching birds, and working. Or was there?

The door jingled as an old couple came in. She knew them from other times they'd visited the store. Yeller's tail thumped in welcome, but he stayed on his rug behind the counter.

She asked, "Can I help you with anything?"

"Fifty pounds of sunflower seed." The old man looked at his wife. "Anything else this young lady can get us, sweetheart?"

"Ten pounds of thistle seed," the old woman piped up.

Joan carried the seed to their car and put it in the open trunk, wondering if they would be able to get it out, and then she saw the woman behind the wheel. Surely she would help.

The couple moved slowly around the store, admiring the feeders, the bat and bird houses, the bird fountains. A good half hour passed before their driver came into the store.

"Mom, Dad, what are you doing?" she asked.

"Looking, honey," the old woman said, taking the younger woman by the arm. "This is our daughter, Linda."

"Hi, Linda. I'm Joan." She shook Linda's hand as the younger woman looked at her with an unreadable expression. "Nice parents," she added.

The woman laughed. "They drive me nuts. They go into a store and disappear for hours."

"We've only been here a short while," the old lady said. "You should come in with us."

The old man said nothing. He continued wandering with his hands clasped behind his back.

"Mom, Dad, the roofer is coming this morning. Remember?"

"I didn't call him," her mother said.

"I did, Mom. He's going to give me an estimate. Remember? You said you only needed birdseed."

Joan almost felt sorry for the younger woman, who was trying so hard to maintain her composure. "Are you a birder?" she asked.

The woman threw her such an annoyed look that she lost any empathy she had. "I like the birds, but I don't go around glued to binoculars."

It was sort of like a slap in the face. She had been thinking that the younger woman was cute: tall and willowy with dark brown eyes and hair. But the crack about binoculars silenced her.

The old man wrote a check in spidery handwriting for the birdseed. When he handed it to Joan, he said, "She's not as ornery as she sounds."

She laughed. "I believe it." She remembered her own parents, who hadn't gotten old enough to tax her patience. The mother and daughter had gone out the door. Through the window, she saw the younger woman opening the door for her mother.

He leaned over the counter. "That your dog?"

"Yes. That's Yeller."

Yeller lifted his head and looked at them with soulful eyes while banging his tail on the floorboards.

"Getting old's not much fun, is it, fella?" the man said. "We lost our dog in January."

"I'm sorry," she said. "What kind of a dog was it?"

What would she do when Yeller died?

"A smart, little dog. The missus and I still miss him."

"Have you thought about getting another?" she asked.

"It's hard to replace a dog like that."

The door jangled, signaling Linda's return. "Are you ready, Dad?" She looked at her watch.

The old man winked at Joan and said to his daughter, "Here I come, honey, ready or not."

Linda held the door open for him, and he shuffled a little faster.

"Don't let the heat in," he said.

"I love the heat," Joan said. "Come again soon."

"When we have more time," he answered.

Linda gave Joan an exasperated look before closing the door behind them.

"Over her dead body," Joan said. "Right, boy?" She bent over and patted the dog and wondered if his tail was callused under the hair from all the pounding.

She went out to fill the tube feeders that hung from a shepherd's crook on the strip of grass between the sidewalk and street. She also put out a birdbath so the birds would have access to water. At night she carried everything inside. The feeders and bath attracted sparrows and finches and a few chickadees. Squirrels spent hours trying to circumvent the baffle. The birds and squirrels provided her with entertainment during slow times. Several times a day she went outside to sweep up the scattered seed.

Once a week she drove to the library and always brought a book to read for when no one was in the store. Sometimes she became so involved in what she was reading that only the jangling door brought her back to reality.

At noon, when no one was in the store, she locked up and took the dog for a relief walk in the empty lot next door. A blast of hot air greeted them when they stepped outside. The building was the last in a strip mall. The field was littered with emptied food containers from the McDonald's on the corner. The grass was sparse, the ground hard and rutted. Dandelions and wild mustard and sweet clover and one honeysuckle bush gave the lot some color. A cloying sweetness mixed with the rank smell of weeds.

As she was returning to the building, a Ford Taurus wagon pulled in and a man got out and strode to the door of Birds of a Feather. She stepped up her pace, breaking into a jog and waving at him. He stood with hands on hips, grinning at her.

"Lunch break?" he asked as she unlocked the door. "Mine too."

Inside the shop was cool, although she turned the air conditioner to its lowest setting. She had never been fond of shutting herself inside a refrigerator. She much preferred open windows and fresh air, even if it was hot. However, as Kathy pointed out, she had to consider the customers.

"Can I help?" she inquired.

He was what she'd call average looking. His features were even, his eyes a muddy brown color, his receding hair a dishwater blond. He was not much taller than she and was neither heavy nor thin. His tie was pulled loose, and he wore his shirt unbuttoned at the collar and tucked into baggy slacks. She was sure there was a blazer thrown over a seat in his car.

"I came to pick up some bird ornaments," he said, smiling easily. He patted the dog, who was nosing around his crotch.

She lifted the box and put it on the counter. "Come lie down, Yeller."

"He's not bothering me. Looks like a great dog. They always want to whiff embarrassing places, though, don't they?"

She laughed. "He should know better."

Yeller thumped down on his rug at the snap of her fingers.

"Hey, I've got a dog who needs to learn to do that. Could I pay you to teach him?" He leaned on the counter as she removed the bird ornaments from the box.

She let the question go, sure that he didn't mean it.

He picked out a nuthatch, a cardinal, a chickadee, a great blue heron, and a goldfinch. "Cute, aren't they?"

She nodded, wondering why he wanted them now.

He told her. "I have a friend who hangs things

from his ficus tree that aren't near as nice as these. They're for his birthday. Think it's a good idea?"

"Sure do," she said, finding him amusing and pleasant.

While he wrote a check, she wrapped the birds in tissue paper and put them in a paper bag.

Getting out his driver's license, he said, "I was serious about the dog training."

"Why don't you take him to dog obedience?" she suggested.

"I have. He's resistant to knowledge; he's also very large. Looks like he's got some shepherd in him without the brains. He drags me around as easy as a horse pulling a buggy."

"I don't have time or I'd consider it. I work two jobs as is."

He put his license back in his wallet. "My number's on the check in case you change your mind." He picked up the bag. "Thanks."

"Thank you," she said, holding his check in one hand.

She looked at it after he was gone. His name was David Ellington, and he lived on the same street as the old man and woman, but in a duplex. She ascertained that from the one-half tacked onto his address. The old couple were Howard and Mildred Brown. How coincidental, she thought, wishing she'd asked him if he knew the Browns. She was intrigued by their daughter.

The rest of the day crawled by, punctuated briefly by regular customers buying birdseed. Between sales, she hunched over her book behind the counter, listening to the hum of the air conditioner. She was reading Ken Follett's book *The Third Twin*, and it was a page-turner.

At five she locked the door behind her, put Yeller in the Bronco, and went to the small Chinese restaurant next door to pick up her food order.

II

At home, she brought in the bag of Chinese carryout and set it on the kitchen table. Then she opened the doors and windows. The smell of honeysuckle and pine needles wafted into the house on a warm breeze, pushing out the stale air that had pooled during her absence. The dog lapped at a bowl of fresh water, gobbled down the dog food Joan poured into his dish and, panting, flopped on the tile floor.

She opened the white containers and spooned the rice and chicken with pea pods onto a plate. Tearing open the plastic bags that held the sweet-and-sour and hot-mustard sauces, she dipped the crabmeat rangoons into the two before popping them in her mouth.

The phone rang, and she let the answering machine pick it up.

"Hey, I know you're there," her boss, Kathy Symington, said. "That's okay. Ignore me. I'm used to it. Just wanted to know how the day went. Give me a call if you're up to it."

The machine clicked and whirred to the beginning of the tape. Joan heard Yeller panting, a cardinal fervently singing outside, and the distant sound of a diesel tractor.

"What do you want to do tonight?" she asked the dog.

He lifted his head and looked at her. His tail thumped.

"As soon as I'm through eating," she said, avoiding the word *walk*. It would excite him prematurely.

They strolled leisurely down the road, Yeller padding along the berm beside her. She would have liked to pick the wildflowers blooming rampant in the ditches: black-eyed Susans, hawkweed, spiderwort, and daylilies. But they grew among dense patches of poison ivy, and she was sensitive to the plant. She saw that the neighboring lot was sold and wished she could pull up the For Sale signs on the other empty lots and trash them, but then thought maybe it would be nice to have neighbors. Sometimes she became nervous at night, aware of her isolation. She and the dog walked to where the tractor traversed the field pulling a cultivator through young corn rows. Swallows dipped and soared over the John Deere in a graceful aerial ballet.

When dusk began its descent, she and the dog

made their way home through the hot, thickly wet evening. Inside, the answering machine blinked its red dot. She turned on lights and pressed the Play button.

"Joanie, give me a call when you get home. Love ya."

It was her oldest friend, Diane, whom she'd known since she was in third grade. Diane and her lover, Tania, were veterinarians in a small-animal practice they operated out of a clinic attached to their house.

"Are you there?" she asked when she got the clinic's answering machine.

Diane picked up the phone. She and Tania screened messages at night so that they could avoid spending all their evenings on the phone. "We're here, we miss you, when are you coming out?"

Whenever she talked to Diane, she wished she had finished her education and amounted to something more than a salesclerk. Maybe she would have had she not married and gone to work to put her husband through law school. He'd offered to do the same for her, but by then she was involved in horses and showing and had lost her interest in higher education. In the end, she sold the horses and left him for a woman. The haphazardness of it all led her to believe that she had been adrift all her life.

Through junior high and high school she had loved Diane passionately. They joined the Girls' Athletic Association and participated in intramural sports. In the locker room she shyly admired Diane's slim body: her small, firm breasts, her slender hips, her muscular legs and buttocks.

Her own body was a little too fleshy even then. At sixteen her fully developed breasts embarrassed her, as did her womanly hips. Her buttocks and legs were too

16

large for her to contemplate. Nevertheless, she had been and was a good athlete as long as she kept her weight under control. Tall and large-boned, she was by normal standards a big woman. Someone had once called her voluptuous, and she caught herself staring in the mirror for weeks afterward, wondering if it was so. Her shoulder length thick hair had been nearly black in her youth. She pulled it back in a loose ponytail or swept it up in a knot if she wanted to look sophisticated. Her eyes were a clear greenish-brown.

"Trixie needs riding. She's getting soft," Diane said. Diane and Tania had taken in Trixie, the mare a large-animal vet had rescued from a life of shocking neglect, when they heard she was going to be put down.

"What Trixie needs is another horse."

Diane and Tania seldom rode, claiming lack of time. Mostly though, they had no passion for the sport. You had to be horse-crazy, Joan thought. Her favorite thing to do was take Trixie down the road with her binoculars around her neck and the dog alongside.

"Trixie has company. The same large-animal vet foisted a pony on us. Poor thing can hardly walk it's foundered so bad."

"You are kind." She meant it. Trixie and the pony were not the only animals the two vets had taken in for various reasons, all of them benign. Kittens and puppies dumped by the side of the road near their clinic ended up being fed and given good homes.

But Diane had no patience with praise. "You would do the same."

Not so, she thought. She'd give any abandoned creatures to Diane or take them to the humane society

17

and pay the donation. "Don't count on it. I'll come out tomorrow. Noonish."

"Stay for dinner."

Next she called Kathy and gave her a rundown on her day at Birds of a Feather.

When she hung up, she said to the dog, "How about some popcorn?"

That got him excited enough to skitter around the kitchen on his toenails for a few minutes.

Settling with the warm bowl in her lap in the old easy chair that had been her parents, she opened her book. While she read, she tossed the waiting dog popcorn, which he caught in midair.

The next morning when she wakened, Yeller was standing by the side of her bed, anxious to be let outside. Pulling a large T-shirt over her nakedness, she padded to the door in her bare feet and opened it to another hot, muggy day, although without sunshine.

It looked and felt like the rainy forecast was going to happen. Damn, she thought, her one day off and it was going to rain. Thunder rumbled in the distance. If she didn't go to Diane and Tania's early, she might not get to ride.

After showering and grabbing a piece of toast, she helped Yeller into the backseat of the Bronco and they drove the few miles to Diane and Tania's clinic. Before they reached the place, she had her usual brief anxiety attack. She still loved Diane. It hurt to see her so happy with someone else.

Yeller stood on the edge of the seat and licked her ear. She saw the dog teetering. If she touched the brakes, he'd fall headfirst onto the floor. "Sit down, Yeller."

And of course he sat.

It made her think of David Ellington. She had nearly called him before Diane phoned her, thinking maybe she'd take him up on his offer and, while training his dog, possibly see the Browns' daughter in the neighborhood. She knew now her name wasn't Linda Brown, because she had looked Brown up in the phone directory. There was only a Lynn, and she reasoned that, because of the roof estimate, Linda didn't live with her parents. Linda could have married, she supposed, and wished she'd looked at her ring finger.

Rounding a curve, she saw the sign in front of the buildings: Oakwood Veterinary Clinic, Diane Russell and Tania Levinsky, Doctors of Veterinary Medicine.

Yeller was standing again, breathing excitedly. He loved this place with its menagerie of animals and open land to run on, although he didn't do much galloping around anymore.

She turned into the large half-circle driveway and parked in front of the clinic. Heat radiated off the blacktop, softening it. Yeller jumped out of the car and quickstepped it to the grass.

Four dogs rushed out of the barn, barking a greeting as they closed the distance. She'd have turned and run had she not known they were all harmless. A buried electric cable, called wireless fencing, prevented them from crossing the drive to the road. The rest of the property was fenced so well that the dogs never ventured outside its boundaries. During the week, they were confined behind closed gates.

She walked up the lane toward the red barn, surrounded by a dog with the head of a Scottie and the long body of a dachshund, a collie mix, a couple of black Lablike dogs, and Yeller. They sniffed under each other's tails and licked snouts. Shoving against her, they looked for pats. Yeller growled an occasional jealous warning.

Diane stepped out of the barn and stood grinning, hands on hips. Joan's heart leaped a little in silent welcome. Still slender and athletic looking, Diane's gray hair blended with the blond so that it all appeared the same color. When she got close, Joan saw the wrinkles that come with age and too much time in the sun. Diane was squinting, shielding her blue eyes from the glare. As teenagers, they'd thought being tan was glamorous and had spent many hours working on darkening their skin.

She enveloped Diane in a hug, inhaling her clean hair along with an overlay of dogs and horses. "As always, you smell delicious," she said.

Diane laughed. Her teeth were straight, her sensuous lips chapped. "Oh sure, if you like the smell of animals."

Putting an arm around her friend, who was nearly the same height, Joan walked with her toward the barn. "Where's Tania?"

"Trimming the pony's hooves. Are you ready for this?"

"That bad, huh?"

They entered the barn, and the sudden change in light temporarily blinded her. The smell here was of hay and horses and manure, odors she sniffed with pleasure. Yeller sat at her side, his tail sweeping a path in the hard dirt floor, ignoring the two cats meowing from the safety of the loft above the stalls.

The pony stood in the crossties. Bent over the animal's foot that she held between her knees, Tania shaved slices off his hoof. He balanced on the other hooves, grown so long that they curled like rockers. His bony back, protruding hips, and shaggy coat told her he'd been starved. Perhaps he'd foundered years ago when he'd got into some corn or something. The equine species would eat themselves to death if given the opportunity. His mane and tail were hopelessly matted with burrs. Her heart went out to him.

"Hi, Tania," she said. "Don't stand up and say hello. I know you're glad to see me."

Tania laughed. "I hope you do know that by now." Tania was ten years younger than Diane. She was short and slender to the point of shapelessness and had curly red hair, green eyes, and lots of freckles. Her puggish nose and large teeth kept her from being pretty, but her kind, friendly, generous nature showed a deeper beauty.

She stood next to Diane, watching Tania trim the pony's feet for a few moments. "Is it hopeless?"

"No," Diane answered. "He'll never be sound, but maybe we can make him comfortable. We have to be so careful not to give him too much to eat too soon."

"I suppose you want to feed him everything he's been denied."

"Like hay and water and grass," Diane said, anger creeping into her voice. "He was found shut up in a dark shed. He'd been eating the studs. There was a tub with a little very dirty water and manure in the bottom."

"You have to wonder, don't you?" she said.

"I'd like to lock up in a windowless basement the person or persons who do stuff like this and only give them enough food and water to keep them alive for a long time."

Joan heard a whinny coming from the field behind

21

her and turned. Trixie stood at the fence, her ears pointed toward the barn. The pony whinnied back, sending hair and dust flying and startling Tania into setting his hoof down.

"They know they're both here. This is what they do all day and night, call back and forth," Tania said, wiping the sweat off her forehead with an arm. She smiled at Joan. "How about a hug? Even if I do stink."

Joan stepped forward to put her arms around Tania, who smelled of sweat and the pony. "Behind the odor is a very nice person. I just have to keep that in mind," she teased.

"Let me finish trimming Shorty's feet before you bring in her highness. He won't stand still if she's around."

When Tania put the pony in a stall, where they had to keep him so he wouldn't eat too much grass, she put a halter on Trixie and led her into the barn. The pony climbed the walls of his stall in excitement at having another of his kind around.

"You'd never guess he's half dead, would you?" Diane said.

"He doesn't know it," Tania concluded. "So how've you been?" she asked Joan.

Joan brushed the chestnut mare and cleaned her feet before putting on blanket, saddle, and bridle. "Just ducky," she said.

The pony called loudly when Joan mounted the mare and left the barn. She took the horse to the large pen outside the clinic. The thunder and lightning had moved closer, and a few drops of rain hit the dusty arena. While Diane and Tania watched, she put the horse through her gaits: walking, trotting, and cantering both ways. Trixie was well broke. She could show her at open horse shows. Diane and Tania would lend her their two-horse trailer. If Trixie had any papers, they'd been lost during the course of her life. Joan couldn't prove her age, much less her breed, which she guessed was mostly quarter horse. At an open horse show that wouldn't matter, as long as it wasn't a class that required registration papers.

She gave the horse a hosing down before putting her back in the field, where the mare immediately rolled, grunting with pleasure. The patter of rain quickened. The three women went into the old farmhouse through the back door.

"God, I love Sundays," Tania said. But the light on their answering machine was blinking. When she pressed Play, David Ellington said his dog had been hit by a car. "You call him, Diane."

"I know him," Joan told Tania while Diane directed him to bring the dog to the clinic so they could look him over.

"He's got the biggest, dumbest dog in the world," Tania said, "but he's a nice guy."

In less than twenty minutes they heard the Taurus's tires protest as David tore into the driveway and parked next to the Bronco. Lifting the dog in his arms, he staggered under its weight toward the clinic. Diane opened the door, and he scrabbled through sideways and set the dog on the examining table.

David was in such distress that at first he didn't notice Joan. "He was chasing a squirrel and ran right out in front of a car. He pulled me off my feet, and I had to let go of the leash."

The animal's coat looked like a German shepherd's, but his ears drooped and he was so big that Joan thought maybe he was part wolf.

"What's his name again?" Diane asked.

"Beowolf, only I spell the wolf part with an *o*, not a *u*."

Aptly named, Joan thought. "Do you call him Beowolf?"

"No, I call him Wolfie." He looked up at her and appeared puzzled. "I know you, don't I?"

She nodded. "Birds of a Feather."

"Yeah." His face lit up. "Now will you train my dog?"

"We'll see," she said evasively.

Diane was looking in the dog's eyes. "He has a concussion. That's why he's so out of it. You two talk while Tania and I take x-rays."

David stepped over to Joan and anxiously watched the two vets maneuver the dog and the x-ray machine.

"Think he'll be all right?" he asked her.

"He looks pretty good." She patted Yeller, who'd sat obediently next to her throughout.

"He does, doesn't he?" he said.

And she wondered why David wanted this dog, who nearly dragged him in front of a moving vehicle, to get well. It was ridiculous the way people loved their pets. "How long have you had him?"

"Got him in January from the Humane Association. They almost didn't let me have him, said he was intractable, but he was still a pup. I gave them references, fenced in the yard, paid to have him neutered, signed up for dog obedience classes. You'd think I was adopting a baby, not a dog that nobody else wanted."

"That's the way they are. You have to be proved responsible."

"Where'd you get your dog?" he asked.

"He was the runt of a litter dumped by the side of the road here. The one Diane couldn't find a home for. That was ten years ago." And before Tania came here to do her internship or residency under Diane's guidance, before they fell in love. Why hadn't she moved on Diane back then?

"There are no broken bones that we can see," Diane said. "But I think we should keep Wolfie here overnight because of the concussion and to watch him for signs of internal injuries."

David laid the dog on a rug in a large kennel and gently stroked him. He drove off after offering many apologies for interrupting their day and giving profuse thanks for taking care of Wolfie on a Sunday.

The women and Yeller returned to the house. Tania popped a cork out of a bottle of ice cold Chardonnay and filled three glasses. She put down water for Yeller, who lapped it greedily.

"So you know David?" Diane asked Joan.

"Met him only yesterday."

"Think seriously about helping him teach that dog some manners before Wolfie accidentally kills them both."

"I am," she said, raising her glass of wine in a friendship toast. But she didn't tell them she was considering it because he lived near Linda's parents. The story was too involved, her hopes too whimsical.

"He's one of us, you know," Tania remarked, taking a seat on the battered sofa next to Diane, who placed a hand on her knee.

"I thought so," she said.

Thunder boomed overhead and a jagged streak of lightning flashed outside the window. The rain turned into a deluge.

"I hope Trixie doesn't get struck." Joan looked outside at the storm with mild alarm.

"She'll be all right. She doesn't have to stand under a tree." There was a shed in the field.

III

Yeller was a fixture at the feed mill. His rug lay behind the counter there, too, on the uneven plank floor. The building was old, turn of the century, built along a creek that once turned a huge paddle wheel to grind the grain. The wheel was for looks now. Behind the feed mill spread a mill pond, dammed to supply fast water.

Farmers brought their grain to dry in the huge blue dryers or to sell after it had been dried. The trucks drove onto the scales full and, after dumping their loads, weighed in empty. Joan wrote out the weigh tickets and also worked up front, selling feed and seed and fertilizer and other farm-related items. There were halters, lead ropes, corner feeders, portable stalls and gates, worming products, animal clippers, and whatever else an animal owner might need or want.

She liked the smell of Taggart's Breed and Show, the feed the mill mixed and tagged as its own. Diane and Tania bought the bagged feed for Trixie. Her shiny coat showed the quality of the mix.

Joan had hung feeders from the overhang on either side of the Taggart's Feed Mill sign and filled the feeders daily. Because of the nearby water and cover, they lured to the hanging platform a larger variety of birds — cardinals, blue jays, nuthatches, woodpeckers, and sometimes rose-breasted and evening grosbeaks — than the ones at Birds of a Feather. The tubes attracted chickadees and hordes of finches.

Sunshine filtered through the dusty windows, exposing the motes always floating in suspension. She leaned on the counter, her chin in her hands. It was only eight A.M. on a Monday, usually a quiet time except during planting and harvesting. Yeller slept on his rug at her feet. The rain the night before had rid the air of humidity. Although the thermometer was climbing toward eighty, the air felt cool. She heard the water falling over the dam, saw from the side windows its spray turned by the sun into tiny rainbows.

That was when Linda stepped through the door dressed in a dove-gray pantsuit and a white blouse. She carried a briefcase. Joan thought at first she was imagining what she wanted to see. Maybe she wouldn't have to work with David Ellington's dog to see this woman after all.

Linda smiled, and Joan found herself staring at her mouth and thinking, lovely teeth, great lips. Were her own teeth free of toast crumbs? She squelched the urge to gallop to the bathroom and grin in the mirror.

Straightening up, she said, "Can I help you?" It was like déjà vu.

The woman looked startled. "We've met, haven't we?" she said.

"Birds of a Feather," Joan explained.

"Ah yes." Linda's brown eyes cleared and she sighed. "I was a little impatient that morning."

"You were meeting with a roofer. Did you get home in time?"

"Yes, I did." The woman chewed on her lower lip as if distressed.

"Not good news?" she asked.

Linda said crisply, "I have to have a new roof, but it's all taken care of."

"How are your parents?" She had a million questions.

An impatient look crossed the woman's face. "Fine. I'm here to see the manager. Would you tell him Linda Brown-Wirtz is here?"

"Sure." Jim Taggart was in the mill, filling feed bags. She switched on the interbuilding speaker and called him to the front of the store.

Yeller raised his head and got to his feet. He yipped, and Joan jumped at the sound. He had been having trouble getting up for some time, but until now he'd never acted as though it hurt. Padding out from behind the counter, he wagged his tail at Linda.

Linda stepped toward him and stroked his head. "What a nice dog. What is he?"

"I'm guessing he's part yellow Lab and part golden

retriever. Your dad said they lost their dog last winter, that they still miss it."

Another shadow crossed Linda's face. "He was a great little dog. Smart as they come." She looked at Yeller. "Is he yours?"

She nodded. "He was behind the counter Saturday. You didn't stay long enough to see him."

"Don't make me feel any guiltier than I do," she said. "I love my parents. I hate it when I lose patience with them."

Jim strode through the door separating the store from the mill part of the building. "How are you, Linda?" He wiped his hand on his overalls before offering it. Hers disappeared in his as he turned to Joan. "Linda handles the Hurtz products. Joan takes care of everything up front."

Joan extended a hand. Although Linda's hand was soft, her grip was surprisingly strong and Joan found herself squeezing back with perhaps too much force.

Jim said, "Come on into the office. You, too, Joan. Joan knows more about what sells than I do."

They went into the windowed office behind the counter. Yeller followed. Jim sat in the chair behind the desk, and the two women took the seats on the other side.

"You've got some new products, I understand?"

Linda pulled a pair of glasses out of her jacket pocket and put them on before taking some brochures out of the briefcase. "As I told you, we've taken over the Furman line. You might be interested in their complete line of animal products, from dog collars to cow and horse halters and sheep shears, as well as pig prods." She placed the written information on the desk along with a sheet with cost figures and suggested selling prices.

After adding a few new products to their present standing order, Jim went back in the mill and Joan stood with Linda in the middle of the store.

"Why haven't I met you here before?" Joan asked.

"I sell mostly over the phone. Jim prefers it that way. This time he asked me to come out and show him the new product line." Linda put her glasses back in their case in her pocket.

"Will you be coming out again?"

"Probably not. Orders can be taken care of by phone or fax." Linda hesitated. "Nice to see you again."

Then the woman was gone before Joan could think of anything else to say that would detain her.

"Well, buddy," she said to the dog, "tonight we call David Ellington."

"Joan?" the voice said. "David here. You left a message on my machine. Sorry I was out."

The windows were black with night. She'd phoned him around seven.

"I hope ten's not too late to call."

She was reading in bed. An earthy breeze drifted inside through the wide-open windows. "I'm awake. How's Wolfie?"

"I picked him up tonight. He's rather subdued. Do you think dogs learn by their mistakes?"

"Sometimes." She heard Dave Brubeck's "Take Five" in the background.

And a male voice was second-guessing David, saying, "Not Wolfie. He's dumb as a box of rocks."

"Do you still want me to help you with Wolfie?" she said.

"Would you? I'll pay you well."

"How well?" she asked. It had to be worth her while.

"You name it."

"Ten an hour," she said, "and that includes getting there."

"Done," he replied. "When can you start?"

"After work Tuesdays and Thursdays, starting tomorrow."

"You have my address?" he asked.

"Yep. I know right where you are."

She drove there after work, stopping only to take Yeller home and grab a sandwich. The dog looked at her wistfully as she locked him in the house with the air conditioner running. She drove off feeling guilty.

The duplex where David lived was two doors from the small apartment building that housed Linda's parents. She had written down both addresses. The neighborhood was a mix of apartment buildings and duplexes. David's duplex was two stories with a high fence around the backyard. The front was landscaped for privacy. Tall, half-shuttered windows hid behind yews, and a row of bridal wreath and snowball bushes separated the yard from the neighbors. Brick walkways curved toward the front doors. She rang the doorbell and heard its tones resonating, followed by the deep barking of a dog.

David flung open the door to her. "Come on in."

Stepping inside, she thought she heard Wolfie's body hit a door and braced herself. "Where is he?"

"Out back."

She had brought a pinch-type choke collar with her, its links designed to cut off breathing if the dog pulled against it and to release as soon as the animal backed off. That always got a dog's attention.

David opened the back door carefully, one hand ready to grab the dog. "He won't hurt you, but he'll jump on you."

She found herself sitting on the kitchen floor with Wolfie in her lap. Slipping the choke collar over the dog's head, she fastened the six-foot leather lead to it while she and the animal were face-to-face.

"I'm sorry," David apologized. "I don't know how to keep him from leaping at people. He's so glad to see everyone."

Joan handed him the leash and got to her feet. "Knee him in the chest whenever he jumps at you, that's how. Maybe we should work in the backyard for a while."

Flower beds separated the grass from the wood fence that shielded the backyard from the other half of the duplex as well as from the surrounding properties. A brick patio with a grill and lawn furniture stood outside the door, and a porch off one of the rooms offered shade overhead. Most of the flower beds lay in ruins, either crushed by the dog's weight or cratered by holes the animal had dug.

"I wish you could have seen the flowers before Wolfie arrived," David said wistfully. "They were lovely."

Positioning the dog on her left, Joan told Wolfie twice to sit before jerking him into position. Wolfie yipped with surprise and sat on his haunches, slowly, as large dogs do.

David bit his nails. Seeing his concern, Joan said, "He's too strong for a regular choke collar; the pinch collar gets his attention."

Then she commanded, "Wolfie, heel," and marched around the yard, jerking whenever the dog lagged. The animal was dangerously strong, his neck thick and muscular. He could have dragged her anywhere. The trick was to fool him into thinking she was in command and to make him want to please her. She patted and praised him whenever he did something right. At the end of forty-five minutes, she was exhausted.

"Let's stop now, while I'm still in control."

David shut the dog outside with a bowl of dog food to distract him, and offered her a drink.

"You earned it," he said, taking a pitcher of margaritas out of the fridge. "Do you think he's trainable? My roommate says he's not."

"I thought he was lightening up toward the end."

He set out a plate of chips and salsa and pulled out a chair at the table for her. "What does that mean?"

She sat down and looked out the window at Wolfie, who was standing on hind legs, staring in at her out of yellow eyes. "He wasn't pulling so hard, like maybe he was getting the idea."

"God, I hope so. Guy says he's moving out if this doesn't work. How do you know so much about training dogs?"

"Years ago I helped teach dog obedience." When Yeller was a puppy, she'd gotten involved enough to offer her services. It seemed she had a knack for getting a dog to want to work for her. She was strong and patient and determined.

The front door opened and a male voice called, "I'm home." Footsteps headed their way.

"Guy Logan, this is our fairy godmother, Joan McKenzie." David poured a third margarita. "Sit down." He patted the chair between them.

"The goddamn wolf is looking in the window." Guy was short and broad shouldered with a black crew cut, thick eyebrows that met over his nose, and a heavy shadow where his beard was growing back. His teeth were long, his lips and nose thick, his ears close to his head. "Are you going to rescue us from this four-legged psychopath?"

"I'm going to try," she said with a grin.

He slid into the chair and took a long swig of his drink. "Thanks, Dave. You're a good man, but you may have to choose between me and that animal."

She stifled a laugh. When she finished the margarita, she said she had to leave, her dog was waiting.

"What's your dog like?" Guy asked.

David answered for her. "He's a big old dog with elegant manners. You could take him to anyone's house."

"Want to trade?" Guy offered. He gestured at Wolfie, who had dropped to all fours and was barking at the closed back door. "Can we keep him outside until he's civilized?"

On her way out she noticed the ficus tree in front

of the living room window, the birds hanging from its branches. She smiled and nodded at it.

"He loved them," David said, opening the front door for her.

Before going outside, she asked, "Do you know the Browns? They live in the apartment house two doors down."

"I don't know anybody in the neighborhood. Are they friends of yours?"

"Actually, they're a really nice old couple I met at Birds of a Feather. Their daughter was with them. I saw her again Monday at my other job."

"Ah," he said as if he understood, but he appeared puzzled. "It's the daughter who interests you. Maybe I do know them. What does she look like?"

"Tall and slender, brown hair and eyes."

"I think I met them on Sunday when my dog ran out in front of her car. Was it a Grand Am?"

"Yeah," she said, "a red one."

He went outside with her. It was nearly dusk, the light from the setting sun was as soft as the air, and a cardinal was singing its heart out in one of the bushes. Streetlights came on as they stood near the Bronco. Little kids rode their tricycles up and down the sidewalks. Older kids threw a football in the street. Someone was mowing a lawn across the road.

She looked toward the Browns' apartment building and briefly thought of visiting them. She could walk over there and ring their bell, but would they remember her? And what would she say to them?

"I should apologize to them," he said. "I was so upset. It wasn't their fault."

* * * * *

36

At home Yeller met her at the door. He gave her a little grin, showing his front teeth, and wagged his tail in welcome.

"You sweet old thing," she said. "What would I ever do without you?"

The answering machine blinked at her in the dark room. She sat down next to it and patted the dog while she replayed its message.

She'd left her purse at David's. She should never have taken it out of the car. He offered to drop it off at Birds of a Feather, but she wouldn't be there till Saturday. She picked up the phone and told him she'd come get it right away.

Yeller stuck his head out the rear window, his ears flying, his long tongue hanging out as she drove to the duplex.

David met her at the door with the purse. As she walked around the Bronco to get back inside, the Grand Am passed her and drove into the apartment building parking lot. Jumping into her vehicle, she arrived in the lot as the Browns got out of the car. Linda was standing with them on the blacktop under a dusk-to-dawn light. The three of them stared at her with obvious surprise.

"Hi, how are you?" she asked, feeling foolish.

"Well, it's the young lady from the bird store," the old man said. "Do you live around here?"

"No," she explained, turning and pointing down the street. "I'm helping David Ellington with his dog."

"That's the dog you hit the other day, Linda," the old lady said. "We offered to take it to the veterinarian, but the young man was so undone he hardly looked at us. How is it?"

"He had a concussion, but he's fine now. David

said it wasn't your fault, that he was sorry the dog ran into your car."

"Like he was bent on suicide," Mr. Brown said.

"Well, he's a little out of control. That's why David asked for my help."

"You're a dog trainer too?" Linda's mother asked.

"Not really. It's something I used to do." Their faces were barely visible under the light, but she sensed their bewilderment and felt awkward. "I just wanted to say hello." Backing toward the Bronco, she bumped into it. Yeller panted in her ear and then licked her cheek.

IV

During the next two days, she blushed whenever she thought of pursuing Linda's car into the apartment parking lot. She had found Linda's name and address in the phone book and driven past the place Wednesday night. The ranch-style brick house was across the street from a park that fronted the river.

She and Yeller had sat on a bench and watched the water hurtle past. The ducks and geese that had flown off at their approach muttered and honked in protest, chasing one another bad temperedly across the surface of the water. The setting sun had laid a dark red sheen over the river, which faded to dusky rose and then to black. With their lights on, boats of all sizes made their stately way downriver toward their moorings. It would be a nice place to live, she'd thought as she and Yeller had climbed into the Bronco for the drive home.

After leaving the feed mill Thursday, she drove Yeller home again before going to the duplex to work with Wolfie. When she had Wolfie under better control, she'd take Yeller with her to teach Wolfie to mind her even when distracted by the presence of another dog.

David let her inside. As they walked toward the kitchen, she saw Wolfie leaping at the window. His dirty paws made random marks on the glass, abstract art by a dog out of control.

"I think I'll take him out front and work him on the sidewalk," she said. "He's never tried to bite anyone, has he?"

"No. But if it weren't for you, I'd have to take him back to the Humane Association. He pays no attention to me."

"First, let me see you work him," she said as he opened the back door.

Wolfie failed to knock her over this time; she was ready. When he launched himself toward her, she kneed him in the chest. While he was catching his breath, she slipped the choke collar on and handed the leash to David.

"Jerk, hard," she said as the dog dragged him around the yard. "Let's go out front. I'll take him for a while."

She pulled the dog up short too many times to

count, and he still took off when she let up on the leash. Handing David the leash again, she told him to show no mercy, then leaned against the Bronco and coached.

Out of the corner of her eye, she saw the old couple emerge from the apartment building and head their way. They walked arm and arm. Before they reached David and the dog, who was straining toward them in welcome, they started to cross the street.

"Hi," she yelled, and they looked her way and paused.

"That the bird lady?" the old man said.

"Yeah. My name's Joan." She couldn't recall whether she'd introduced herself.

"Heel," David shouted. "Damn it, heel."

The dog wheezed as he leaned into the choke collar. Joan went over and jerked him to a sitting position.

David tied him to a sapling between the sidewalk and the curb and walked with her to the old couple. "Sorry about the dog. You were in the car that he ran into, weren't you?"

"Our daughter's car," the old lady said.

"If there was any damage to it, my insurance will pay," David offered. "Hitting Wolfie is like hitting a deer."

"Don't think the car was hurt any. Scared us, is all. We'll ask her when we go out for fish tomorrow," the old man said.

"Where do you go?" Joan asked.

"Rounders." The woman's smile was friendly.

The old couple crossed the street and threaded their way through the tricyclers, then rounded a corner and disappeared.

"Want to go out for fish tomorrow night?" David asked.

When she got home, she phoned Diane and Tania even before switching on a light. Sitting down while the ringing echoed in her ear, she absently played with Yeller's ears and felt his tongue on her wrist. David had pointed out that the Browns probably went early to eat.

"Pick it up," she said when she got the answering machine. "I need a favor."

"What?" Diane asked.

"I met this woman," she began, and told her what there was to tell about her encounters with Linda.

"I can't promise we'll be able to get away from here by five-thirty. We might get tied up."

"I know. David has offered to go with me, but I wanted your opinion."

"You don't know if she's a lesbian?"

"Who gives out that information?" she said defensively. "Do you go somewhere and admit you're a lesbian?"

"Only if I'm asked," Diane teased. "Look, sweetie, we'll meet you at Rounders as close to five-thirty as possible. Take David up on his offer."

"I already have. Wolfie has driven his roommate out of the house." David had told her Guy had even taken his ficus plant.

When she hung up, she opened all the windows and sat in the dark, absently stroking Yeller and remembering her only woman lover. She and Yeller had lived in a shabby apartment complex near Birds of a Feather with Mary and her cat.

She tried to conjure up an image of Mary and failed. She had been taken in by Mary's easy charm and only later realized there was nothing behind the charisma. Mary was always looking for something or someone to fill her needs. Unable to find satisfaction in her own life, she sought it from outside. She was forever buying things, which she'd use a few times and then put in the garage to gather dust: a bike, Rollerblades, skis.

At first she'd been crazy about her, wild with desire for her, and chased her till she succumbed, thinking that once would satisfy her. Of course, it only fed her need. Less than a year into the relationship, Mary was cheating on her. She realized now that Mary's desire for another woman stemmed from the same inner emptiness that fed her need for new things. But Mary also had had trouble letting go of the old. Freeing herself had initiated for Joan a depressing struggle that ended in bitterness.

She entertained a dismaying thought: She might be pursuing another woman like Mary or, worse, a woman who wasn't gay.

Laying out slacks and a short-sleeve shirt for a quick change after work the next night, she went to bed early with a book.

The following morning she wakened with the first stirring of birds. Glancing at the clock, she saw it was four-thirty. At five she gave up trying to sleep and dressed to run. With her binoculars around her neck and Yeller at her side, she jogged the three miles of road that squared her property. The red, orbed sun rose over the trees and the waning moon hung low in the western sky. Along the roads, grass and flowers strung together by spider webs spun during the night glistened with dew. She heard only the dog panting, her own labored breathing, her feet hitting the blacktop, and birds singing as she passed. Occasionally, when she noticed an unfamiliar song, she stopped to find the bird through her binoculars.

At home, she and Yeller showered. He loved the cascading water and turned his long, blunt nose upward with tongue out to catch the drops. The shower was a double walk-in with tile walls and floor. She covered the drain with a piece of hardware cloth to catch the hair. The only time she allowed him to bathe with her was after a run or a walk when he was either hot or dirty. And she never told anyone.

When she and Yeller unlocked the feed store and walked inside, Jim said, "Looks like you both showered this morning."

"I hosed him off," she lied. "We went for a run."

"I see one of the lots next to yours sold," he said.

"Do you know who bought it?"

"Nope." And he disappeared through the back door into the mill.

Around noon Diane came in to pick up grain and dog food. "Brought lunch." She gave the bag to Joan to pop in the microwave oven. "Tuna casserole. Nothing exciting."

When they sat down to eat, she said, "Diane, do you remember when we were kids and you wanted to grow up to be a veterinarian, which you did?"

Diane nodded around a mouthful of casserole.

"What did I want to be?"

After she swallowed, Diane said, "You wanted to be a horse trainer, and you were for a while. You also worked with dogs."

She snorted sarcastically. "I had a couple of horses I showed, and I helped with dog obedience classes."

"How is Scott anyway? Do you ever see him?"

Scott was Joan's ex-husband. Happily married, he was, at the age of forty-nine, the father of twin six-year-olds. "He does my taxes and advises me on my finances when I ask."

"What's wrong, Joan?"

She shrugged. "I'm restless. I feel like I've frittered my life away." She looked at Diane imploringly. "And here are you with a DVM degree and a successful business."

"Why don't you go into business for yourself?" Diane asked.

"Doing what?"

"Training and boarding dogs, grooming maybe."

She envisioned nights made sleepless by barking, evenings spent jerking dogs like Wolfie around, days filled with washing and clipping unappreciative four-legged clients. "I'd never be able to go anywhere, and I spent my nest egg on a down payment for the house. There's nothing left." She felt like crying.

"Look, sweetie," Diane said, "having your own business is not all its cracked up to be, and you're right, it does tie you down. You also have to provide for your own retirement and pay your own insurance, while working your butt off trying to make ends meet. There is only you to fall back on." Diane glanced at her watch. "Got to go. Tania will be at her wit's end."

Joan helped load the bags of feed and watched Diane drive off. "I should have married her," she said to Yeller, who stood on the porch with her under the overhang. "Then I could be her assistant."

The afternoon turned into a stream of customers picking up feed. The bags weighed fifty pounds each, and most clients bought a thousand pounds at a crack. The phone rang so much that Jim came out front to help her with the loading.

She didn't get away till well after five, and she sped home through the golden afternoon. The day had been hot, and she was layered with sweat and the dust of feed that had seeped out of the bags.

As she fishtailed into her driveway, she passed a truck and trailer with a backhoe on it parked along the roadside. A man dropped the ramps and drove the Case off the trailer and up into the next-door lot where he turned it off. She had no time to stroll over there and talk to him as she wanted. Maybe he would be around tomorrow.

Jumping into the shower, she washed the dust from the feed mill off her skin and hair. After drying her hair and tying it back, she put on the slacks and shirt, looked up the address for Rounders, and got back in the Bronco. The truck and trailer were gone.

Rounders was on the access road, and the rear end of the Bronco skidded sideways when she pulled onto the gravel of the parking lot. Twice in one night meant she was in too much of a hurry. She saw David's Taurus parked nearby and looked around for the red Grand Am. Perhaps it was on the other side of the building.

She strode toward the building and threw open the

door. David was perched on a stool in the bar. She caught sight of him as she passed by on the way to the hostess. Backing up, she went up to him and tapped him on the arm.

He followed her into the lobby. "I was striking up a conversation with a truck driver."

"Was he cute?" she asked. "I didn't notice."

"Hairy and big bellied. I guess you saved me."

After telling the hostess they were waiting for friends, they went back into the noisy, smoky bar and found an empty table next to the windows. She ordered a glass of Merlot. Outside was a fenced-in terrace set with tables for dining and lit by strings of tiny white lights.

"Let's eat out there," she suggested.

"The Browns are here," he said.

She felt her face grow hot. "Where?"

He smiled and nodded discreetly. "There."

She turned in time to see Mrs. Brown wiggle her fingers in a wave. "Let's go say hello."

"I did. I'll wait here. The truck driver is giving me the eye again. Hurry back."

With her heart hammering at her ribs, she started toward the table where the mother, father, and daughter were seated. "We decided to give this place a try. Any hints on what to order?"

"The perch is good," Mr. Brown said.

"The combo is better," his wife told her.

"What about you?" she asked Linda, looking for her ring finger.

Linda's hands were in her lap. "Haddock."

"Would you like to join us?" Joan asked. "We're waiting for a couple of friends."

"Thank you, dear." Mrs. Brown smiled at her. "But we're waiting for friends too. I'm afraid it might require a banquet table."

David raised his glass in a toast to the Browns as she turned from their table. In her nervousness she hooked a chair leg with her foot. Recovering her balance, her face livid with color, she stammered a good-bye.

"They must think I'm a fool," she said, swallowing a gulp of wine and then choking.

He patted her on the back. "Tripped up by a chair," he said, bursting into laughter. When he could talk again, he told her about trying to impress someone and falling on his face. "At least you didn't do that." It was small comfort.

When Diane and Tania arrived, looking flushed and hurried, the Browns had met their friends and had been seated in the dining room.

"Someone dumped another three puppies at our door," Diane said. "We must have been showering. We had to feed and water everything before we could leave, that's why we're late." She looked around. "Where is this woman you find so interesting, Joan?"

It was nearly seven, and Joan was flushed and a little high from wine and lack of food. "They're in the dining room. Do you want to eat there or outside?"

"Whichever is quicker. I'm starved," Tania said.

They were shown to a table on the terrace, where the scent of roses hung heavy in the warm evening air. Sitting on the sun-warmed chair, Joan saw they faced the dining room and the Browns' table. She blushed when Mrs. Brown again waggled her fingers at her.

"That her?" Diane asked. "The one with the long, brown hair?"

"Yep," Joan answered. The Browns had been joined by another elderly couple accompanied by a younger woman. "I played volleyball with that other woman last summer. Can't remember her name."

"Joanie, I've introduced you to friends who've slavered over you. Why didn't you find one of them interesting?"

Maybe she was like Mary, always dissatisfied, always looking for the elusive.

"Tell us about the puppies." David leaned on the table.

"Little fur balls. I don't know how anyone could part with them," Tania said.

"Maybe you'd trade one of them for Wolfie."

Tania smiled a little. "The dogs at our place have to coexist."

Diane was sipping a glass of Chardonnay and obliquely studying Linda Brown-Wirtz. "I haven't a clue, Joanie. I can't tell by looking at her."

"They both are," David said, following her gaze. "I've seen them at Diversity." He called the waitress over and ordered another beer. "I didn't know you thought she might not be one of the club."

V

They left long after the Browns did and drove to Oakwood Clinic to see the dumped puppies. Their arrival set up a din of barking, and Joan thought this would be what it would sound like to run a kennel.

The puppies, all pitch-black with curly hair and tails, rolled around the cool clinic floor. Joan picked one up and held it close. The pup chewed on her fingers and wriggled high in her arms, attempting to lick her face.

"I bet Guy would come back to me if I had one of

these instead of Wolfie. You sure you wouldn't consider a trade?"

Tania said with a corroborating glance at Diane, "Bring Wolfie out and see how he behaves. Perhaps he just needs a place to run."

"There goes my part-time job," Joan said.

"You already work two jobs," Diane pointed out.

The next morning Joan woke early but decided she was too thickheaded to go for a run or a walk. Returning to sleep, she dreamed that a train was coming toward the house and that she was too sluggish to get out of bed in time to escape. Yeller yipped at her, but she just couldn't open her eyes.

When she climbed out of sleep, Yeller was standing with paws on the window ledge, barking at the Case backhoe in the lot next door. His deep woof sounded like the word.

"Yeller, hush," she said. He dropped to the floor, looking abashed. "Come here."

He lumbered over to her, and she put her arms around his thick body. "What's going on, anyway?"

Getting out of bed, she saw that the backhoe was digging a trench next door — a finger system, she supposed. They'd be starting construction soon.

Padding into the kitchen, she put on the coffee and went into the bathroom to shower. She dressed in lightweight slacks and a T-shirt that said Wisconsin Backyard Birds on the front. After eating a couple of pieces of toast and giving Yeller the ends, she slipped on her Birkenstocks and meandered next door.

Raising her cup of coffee to the man on the backhoe, she mouthed the words, "Want some?"

He nodded and pulled the fuel knob, shutting off the tractor. The sudden silence gave way to blue jays screeching in the woods, a breeze whispering in the trees. He jumped off the deck of the tractor.

"Name's Lou Parry," he said, extending a hand. "Thought I'd get an early start. Hope I didn't wake you up."

"I needed waking up. I have to leave for work soon. I'll be right back with the coffee."

She poured him a cup. When she returned, he was leaning against the rear tire of the Case, patting the dog.

"We're going to be neighbors, huh?" he said, taking the steaming cup from her.

"I thought you were working for whoever bought the land."

He was shorter than she was and had wispy blond hair and slightly crossed blue eyes. Chest hair sprouted out of his ragged T-shirt and hairy legs from his khaki shorts. "The land's mine. I borrowed the backhoe from the construction firm where I work."

"In some ways it'll be nice to have a neighbor," she said.

He laughed. "That's honest enough. Actually, I'll probably sell the house after it's built. I do this on the side." Yeller leaned against him. "Nice dog."

"He likes you. That's a good sign." Unusual, too. Yeller was friendly, but he was a one-woman dog. She glanced at her watch. "Gotta go."

When she climbed into the Bronco, the battery made a weak attempt to turn the starter, then gave up. She had to ask Lou for a jump-start. He shut off the Case, drove his truck next to hers, lifted the hood, and attached cables from his battery to hers.

She was sweating when she opened Birds of a Feather, and the phone was ringing. Thinking it would be Kathy, she said, "Hey, friend."

The silence on the other end told her she'd been wrong. "Is this Birds of a Feather?" She didn't recognize the voice.

"Yes."

"How long are you open?"

She gave the hours and hung up, feeling stupid.

Kathy called a few minutes later. "Got an order of feeders yesterday. They're in storage. If you have time, maybe you could put one up for people to see."

"No problem. It'll give me something to do."

She forgot about the feeders until late in the day and was screwing the parts together when the woman who had been sitting with the Browns last night walked through the door. Joan hunkered back on her heels and smiled a little, thinking there had been a lot of coincidences in the past few days.

"Can I help you with anything?"

"Just browsing," the woman said. "Don't I know you?"

"Volleyball last summer," Joan replied, remembering the woman was a terrific player. She had the build for it: tall, broad shouldered. "Sorry, I can't remember your name." She got to her feet. "Mine's Joan McKenzie."

"You came with Mary what's-her-name." The woman snapped her fingers.

"Yep. Old Mary what's-her-name. Haven't seen her since we stopped playing volleyball." Actually, that was why she had quit, to get away from Mary, and it was one of the reasons why she wasn't playing this summer.

The woman laughed knowingly, mouth open, blue eyes bright, throwing back a head full of brown curls. "Mary's not playing either."

"Well, things change. For the better this time."

"The name's Liz Erickson." She held her hand out. "We could use you on our team. You're a good player."

Joan shrugged. This was the woman who had called early that morning. "I'm too busy. This is a second job."

"Saw you last night at Rounders." Liz started to walk around the room, looking at the merchandise.

"Through the window." Yeller had risen and stood at Joan's side, his head under her hand.

"Nice you can have your dog with you. Linda said she saw him with you at the feed mill."

So Linda had talked about her. It gave her a needed lift. "She's a friend of yours?"

"We've been friends since we were in grade school."

"I have a friend like that." She wanted to ask if Linda was with someone, if she was married, if she went with Liz to Diversity, but she couldn't bring herself to admit her own interest. Since she'd left Scott, she had been struggling with coming out. She knew who she was. Did she have to share the knowledge with everyone? But then, was she ashamed of her sexuality? Is that why she couldn't bring herself to allude to it?

Finally, she said, "Your friend, Linda, does she play volleyball?"

Again Liz threw back her head and laughed. "No,

although she does play a mean game of tennis and is a good golfer. Her ex-husband is the golf pro at one of the country clubs."

"Who's she married to now?" she blurted.

"No one."

She wanted to ask Liz more, but the door jangled as two women walked through it.

"I have to go. See you," Liz said, going out.

Joan watched her drive off and wondered if Liz had stopped only to check her out. She'd bought nothing, but sometimes people came in to look around. Liz's visit, however, had buoyed her spirits, lifting them to a new level. She wondered why.

When the women left, she sat down to read but found she couldn't concentrate.

Just before closing, David showed up. Looking out the window, she saw Wolfie leaping from front to back in the Taurus, barking.

"I can't stay long. I left the car running with the air on."

"I see Wolfie hasn't changed," she said dryly.

"I thought I'd get him more used to the car. I'm taking him out to the clinic tomorrow to see how he gets along with the other dogs."

"You really do want to make an exchange?"

"He'd be happier not being cooped up, and my life will be easier. What I wanted to know was if you'd come along. You're so good with him."

She snorted, but she was in such a good mood that she agreed. "In the afternoon. Yeller and I are going bird watching in the morning."

* * * * *

The sun was above the treetops dispersing the ground fog when she and Yeller arrived at the wetlands Sunday morning. Hers was the only vehicle in the parking lot. Because lately Yeller had been yelping when he hit the ground, she helped him out of the Bronco.

On one of the islands in the swift flowing river, eagles nested. Putting her binos to her eyes, she saw the female sitting on the nest and the male soaring on wind currents high over the river. The two young looked ruffled and nearly as large as their parents.

As she and Yeller made their way down the stairs and along the boardwalk, warblers flitted from bush to bush. Geese and mallards swam and bobbed in the river's current. Squirrels chased each other from tree to tree overhead. The river swept under the boardwalk and swirled around trees. She saw no out-of-the-ordinary birds. The spring migration had gone through.

Except for the wildlife and the rushing river, it was silent. She would probably not return until fall when the birds again passed through on their way south. She climbed the stairs to the Bronco, helped the old dog in, and drove home.

She thought of the tiny creek that flowed through the deep end of her property. It fed a larger stream that emptied into the river and was one of the reasons she'd wanted the place. The creek was maybe two feet wide and cut through thick blackberry bushes at the edge of third growth trees. Poison ivy flourished along its banks, and clouds of mosquitoes bred there. After a severe case of poison ivy in the fall, she had stayed away from the stream.

She thought the creek accounted for the many birds in her yard. She only filled her feeders in the fall, winter, and spring. The birds were there year-round. Early this spring she had put out bluebird houses along the back of the yard. Nearly every one was occupied. There was no need to go anywhere to bird watch. Some days she sat out back and watched the activity through her binos.

As she neared the house, thickly billowing smoke enveloped the Bronco. It gave her a brief scare that it might be her home burning. She parked in front of the garage and heard the irritating buzz of a chainsaw, rising and falling above the steady growl of the Case's diesel engine.

Furious, she clumped over to the neighboring lot. "What the hell's going on?" she yelled at Lou.

He pulled the throttle down to idle and hopped off the machine. "Just clearing and digging, getting ready to build." The chainsaw continued its annoying racket.

"Do you have to burn too?" she asked.

"Got to get rid of some of the brush."

"I left my windows open," she said. "My house'll be full of smoke."

He lifted his hands in a helpless gesture. "Sorry."

Inside, smoke hovered around the ceilings. She closed the windows and turned on the air. Yeller thumped down on the kitchen floor, his tongue dripping onto the floor.

"We'll grab a sandwich and get out of here," she promised him.

Steaming with anger and helpless to do anything about it except run away, she drove to Diane and Tania's. The lightheartedness of yesterday was gone.

In her mind, Lou Parry was destroying the lot next door by indiscriminately cutting brush and trees alike. How many nests had he destroyed, how many birds had choked on the smoke, how much habitat had been cut down? Woodpeckers and nuthatches and little brown creepers fed on the insects in dead and decaying trees and built nests in their cavities. Bats hung in the branches and holes. She had seen raccoons climb out of hollow trees, not to mention the squirrels who wintered in such places and built their nests out of twigs high in the deciduous trees.

David's Taurus wasn't there yet when she parked in the lot in front of the clinic. She and Yeller went to the barn, where she voiced her worries and complaints.

"Maybe you should talk to this Lou Parry, tell him what you've just told us."

"I'm so mad I could spit." She stomped around the aisle of the barn in agitation. Yeller followed her sedately.

"You could learn from your dog," Diane said.

She paused and patted him. "What does he know, or care? I wish I didn't. I should have stayed in town."

The dogs outside set up a chorus of barking.

"I think David's here," Tania said, looking toward the bright sunlight in the doorway.

It was impossible to tell who he was till he stepped inside. "Hi, ladies. Wolfie's in the car. I didn't dare let him out."

"Let's go get him," Diane suggested. "Joanie needs distraction."

"You're laughing and it's not funny," she said sulkily.

"We know it's not funny, but there's nothing we can do about it." Diane encircled Joan's shoulders and urged her forward.

"I put his choke collar and his leash on at home so you could grab him when he gets out of the car, Joan," David said as they walked together toward the parking lot.

"*You* grab him," she said. "He's too strong for me to hold if he makes a break for it."

Wolfie leaped out of the car and was immediately stopped by Yeller, who bit him on the snout. Wolfie groveled in front of the older dog, exposing his throat and whining.

"I'll be damned," Joan said. "He's acting subordinate. This might work after all."

"Except Yeller won't be here to keep him in line," Tania said.

Diane stood with hands on hips, looking at the two dogs and then at the others who were crowded together at the gate, baying. "Well, let's give it a go."

Wolfie dragged David to the gate. The dogs sniffed at each other through the bars. Tania opened the gate, and Wolfie launched himself inside where he cringed in subservience.

When they realized that Wolfie was not going to kill the other animals or be murdered by them, they walked past the pack to the barn.

"He can't get at the horse, can he?" David asked worriedly. "They brought him to the Humane Association because he chased deer."

"None of them can get at Trixie," Tania assured him. "The fence is too high, and it's woven. Trixie'd as soon kick them in the teeth as look at them anyway. They stay away from her hooves."

"I'm going to ride her. We'll see if he leaves her alone," Joan said.

VI

When Joan asked for one of the pups to offer to the Browns, Diane assented but warned her, "The pups aren't pawns, you know."

"They lost their dog last winter. All they can say is no."

Diane squeezed her arm. "You really want to get in right with this woman, don't you?"

"I don't know." They were standing alone outside the barn. Tania and David had gone ahead to the clinic to get the puppies out. She toed the ground.

"Lust? Loneliness?" Diane was smiling.

"I suppose. It's been a long time. She could be a bitch."

"Well, find out first."

At home the fire next door still smoldered, layering the air with an acrid odor. The backhoe was gone, but drainage tile lay curled like a huge, black snake near her lot line next to a pile of stone. Where grass and bushes once grew, there was now furrowed and pitted brown earth. It put her in a foul mood.

She had been planning to sit in the backyard and sip a vodka and tonic with her binos at the ready. Instead, she went inside and started to clean house. Sometimes the boring tasks soothed her.

As she picked up the phone to dust under it, it rang. She dropped it in surprise, and it crashed to the wood floor.

"Goddamn it," she said, picking it up and putting the receiver to her ear. "Did I burst your eardrum?" She expected it to be Kathy or Diane.

"Almost," a woman said, and she recognized the voice. Liz Erickson. "I wondered if you'd like to come over for a game of volleyball and a picnic. Sort of a pitch-in, but I'll provide the food since it's such late notice."

It took her a moment to digest the meaning of the words. She looked at the clock on the mantel. It was four o'clock. "Are you short a player?" she asked, thinking Liz must have looked her up in the phone book.

"It's a women's get-together. Bring the dog." She gave directions and, thinking why not, Joan jotted them down.

Liz lived on the other side of town in an old farmhouse set in the middle of an acre of lawn. In the back where cars were parked stood a rundown barn leaning dangerously to one side. Joan stepped out of the Bronco and released Yeller from the backseat. A volleyball game was in progress on a side lawn, and she walked over.

"Hey, look who's here. We want her on our side." Liz, hands on hips, sleeveless T-shirt clinging to large, sweaty breasts, nylon shorts outlining her buttocks, grinned at her. "Everyone, this is Joan McKenzie."

Joan saw Linda ensconced in a lawn chair on the sidelines. "I'll sit this one out," she said and dropped cross-legged in the grass nearby.

"How are your parents?" she asked for openers.

"Busy." Linda kept her gaze on the game in progress.

Joan cast about for conversation and began to wish she'd joined the volleyball players. Yeller leaned companionably against her left shoulder, and she suddenly remembered the pups. "I have a couple of friends who are vets. People are always dumping puppies at their doorstep. Right now they have some black puppies with a bad case of the cutes that need homes."

"I don't want to be tied down," Linda said, "nor do I want to be walking an animal in the dead of winter."

"Uh, I was thinking about your parents, not you. Of course, if you wanted the pup, you could have it, but they're the ones who lost their dog." She realized she was babbling and clamped her lips shut. She was also sweating, although they were sitting under a tree out of the low-slung sun.

Linda looked at her. "I don't want to seem rude, but why are you so interested in my parents?"

The words slammed into Joan's ego. Although she flushed and her heart raced unhealthily, she managed a shrug. "I like them, and I know what it's like to lose a pet."

"You don't know what it was like for them to lose their dog." Linda took a sip of the Miller Lite she was drinking. She tilted the can toward Joan. "Want one? They're in the cooler."

"Thanks, no." What she wanted to do was go to her car and leave.

"Come on, Joan," Liz hollered. "Game's over. We need you."

She hadn't even noticed. Gratefully, she got to her feet and trotted over to join Liz's side.

"You okay?" Liz asked, pounding her on the back. "Your face is beet red. Too much sun? Can't be too much exercise."

Get me out of here, she thought. But then the game started and it came back to her like riding a bike. As she spiked and volleyed and served with the best of them, she noticed Liz's athletic body transformed into grace by action, her muscular arms and legs and buttocks all working in rhythm.

When the match was over, the women gathered around the cooler. Those who had been watching the game got up to take their turn at the net, except for Linda.

"How about a game of croquet?" Liz suggested. "Linda will whip our butts."

Linda laughed. "As always, you are so eloquent."

Joan had played croquet as a kid and had never considered it a game that required skill. But watching Linda whip through the course in a matter of minutes, using the competing balls when needed for extra strokes and even sending them through wickets so she could play against them again, made Joan realize there could be more to the match than slamming balls through wickets.

After Linda hit the home stake and won, she and Liz and another woman whose name she had already forgotten finished up.

"I'm ready for some food," Liz said, picking up her mallet and ball and carrying them to the dilapidated garage that stood to the side and behind the house. She beckoned to Joan. "Come on inside."

The kitchen of the old house was square with off-white walls and high ceilings, white-painted cupboards, yellow Formica countertops, and an uneven linoleum floor. The glass in the windows over the porcelain sink was wavy with age, as were the windows next to an enamel table that looked out on the driveway and side lawn. A curtain for a door hid a pantry at one end. In the center of the room stood a much used butcher block on legs. Through the open doorway at the other end she saw a dark dining room.

She wondered if Liz had grown up here and asked. A purring gray cat wound around her legs. Yeller was waiting outside.

"Sure did. We had a hundred milk cows and me and my three brothers to help with the chores."

"None of you wanted to farm?" Now she was curious.

"My parents sold the stock and most of the land before they died. They said farming was no way for a girl to make a living, and my brothers wanted none of it. They said they were tired of busting their asses. I bought the property from the estate after my folks died. My grandparents homesteaded here."

"So what do you do?" she asked.

Liz picked up a carrot and bit off the end. "I work for the post office, delivering mail. Gets me outside in the sun and rain and snow."

Linda had taken a platter of snacks to the picnic table out back under a soaring silver maple. She returned to ferry out casseroles and desserts with some of the other women. "Bring the paper plates and napkins, will you, Liz?"

"I brought some chips. I'll get them out of the Bronco," Joan said. The sun hovered above the house and treetops. Yeller greeted her as if he hadn't seen her all day. That was the best thing about dogs, she thought; they were always glad to see you. It didn't matter if you were gone for days or for minutes.

It occurred to her that Liz might want a dog. She had been planning to drop in on the Browns with the puppy in her arms. After what Linda had said today, however, she couldn't do it.

Yeller watched with longing as the food disappeared. Occasionally a chip or piece of meat dropped to the ground and he ambled over to pick it up. He wasn't rude about it like another visiting dog who went expectantly from woman to woman, begging and snatching at crumbs. When the other dog came over to stare at Joan's food, Yeller growled a low warning, and she put a hand on his head to quiet him.

Liz sat down between her and Linda at the picnic table. The bench bowed under the weight of so many people. "We do this every month, traveling from house to house. It's a good way to meet people." She looked at Yeller, lying behind Joan. "Was he always so laid back?"

"Not when he was a pup. I'm surprised you don't have a dog with all this land."

"My dog got hit by a car last fall right out front here. I came home and found him dead. Can't bring myself to replace him."

As color left the sky, bats emerged from the barn, swooping overhead in their nightly foraging. The women who were still there sat in the dark with only the citronella torches at either end of the picnic table to light their faces.

Joan nursed a beer that had turned warm and flat. "Let me help clean up," she said.

"Sure." Liz grinned, her teeth bright in the gloom. "Did you have a good time?"

"Yes. Thanks for inviting me."

"Maybe we can do something between get-togethers." Liz looked her in the eyes and slapped her on the back. Joan realized they were of the same height and build and, because of it, gave the impression of being capable. No man would ever stop to help them change a tire.

At home that night, the lingering, acrid smoke reminded her of the destruction of the land next door, and her foul mood returned.

Liz called her Thursday evening. "I want to see those pups you told Linda about."

"All right," she said. "When?"

"How about tomorrow night? Afterward, we can go out to eat." Liz spoke in a rush as if she'd practiced the conversation in her head and feared rejection.

Joan was flattered. "I'll call Diane and Tania and see if they're going to be around and get back with you."

"Wait. Why don't I pick you up at your place around six anyway? We can go out to eat whether we see the pups or not."

After work Friday, Joan changed into clean clothes and read the paper while waiting for Liz's arrival. Hearing Liz's Ford Explorer turn into the driveway, she patted the dog good-bye and locked the door behind her.

Liz was standing next to the dark green vehicle. "Guess who wanted to come with us?" she said with a hesitant smile.

Linda sat in the front seat. As Joan climbed into the back, she thought about how this woman always made her feel foolish and said, "I thought you had no interest in a puppy."

"Hello yourself," Linda replied. "I don't, actually. I'm going along for the ride."

"Never been here," Liz said as they parked in front of Oakwood Clinic.

Piling out of the vehicle, the other two women followed Joan toward the barn. As always, the dogs rushed out to greet them. This time, though, Wolfie was in the fore. His tongue and ears and tail flopped in the breeze he created. Joan had forgotten his immense size and hesitated long enough to look behind her. Liz and Linda were pressed against the gate.

"They're all harmless," she said, wanting to laugh. "Come on."

Diane and Tania were hurrying toward them,

the dogs panting as they lay in the dust, a robin singing persistently from an electrical wire.

When Liz and Linda emerged from the building, they were talking as old friends do, answering each other's questions before they were finished.

Joan looked up at them. The late-day sun shone directly on their faces and exposed all the lines etched into their skin by its rays and their years. She realized that they were well into their forties. Maybe not the forty-nine years she had reached, but close.

VII

Instead of Rounders they chose Diversity, the gay bar on the south side of town. If not deafening, the music defeated normal conversation; if not lethal, the smoke worked its way into hair, clothes, pores. But the customers were fun to watch and the fish fry was better than good.

A small bar and picnic tables out back — fenced in for privacy — served those who chose to preserve their lungs and hearing. Beds of roses sweetened the night air. Joan sat on one side of the table with Diane and Tania.

"Ever bring your parents here for fish?" Joan asked Linda in fun.

"No. Did you?" Linda shot back.

"Mine were killed eight years ago in a car accident." It had broken her heart, but at least she hadn't watched them wither and die as Diane's mother had done last year.

"My dad died of cancer, my mother of Parkinson's," Liz said with a sad smile. "Not good, clean ways to die."

Diane and Tania said nothing. Joan knew that Diane, whose father had died when she was a teenager, was still mourning her mother. Tania's parents were alive and healthy, but born-again and homophobic. Tania visited them alone in California once a year. A week was all she could tolerate. They would not come to see her as long as she lived with Diane. She did talk to them on the phone once every couple of weeks and came away from those conversations sad and frustrated. She said that she despaired of them ever accepting her as she was.

If parents only knew what an impact they had, but it sometimes seemed to Joan that their importance grew inversely. She had seen it often enough to know that an accepting and loving parent was often slighted in life, while parents who ignored or disapproved of their children were courted by them. She worried that she'd taken her parents for granted. She'd left Scott after their deaths, which sometimes led her to wonder if their dying had freed her to express her sexual orientation.

She looked up as David sat down next to Linda. He wore a silly grin and carried a drink. Guy, right behind him, thumped down on his other side.

"Do you mind?" David said. He introduced himself to Liz and Linda and Guy to everyone. "How are you, ladies?" Leaning over, he shook hands all around.

"How do you like the puppy?" Joan asked.

"He's adorable," Guy said. "I can't keep my hands off him." In his dark, hairy face his smile was wolfish. "I went back to David because of him."

"How's Wolfie?" David asked.

Tania answered. "Happy. The dogs keep each other in line. He did knock Joan down in welcome tonight, though. He hasn't changed that much."

"Knee him," David said with a wink.

"I can't thank you two enough for giving the wolf a home," Guy said. "The animal was incorrigible."

When their plates came, they ordered more drinks and fell on the food with hunger. Joan glanced up and met David's smile. He looked so happy that she was momentarily jealous.

The women sat talking at the table in the cooling night long after David and Guy had finished eating and gone back into the smoke-filled bar. Liz appeared startled when Joan said it made more sense for her to hitch a ride with Diane and Tania, who were standing, ready to leave. Joan's home was on the way to the clinic.

"I thought I'd drop off Linda and take you home," Liz said.

For a moment, Joan hesitated, then decided it was too late to change her mind. Besides, she didn't know if she wanted to deal with whatever Liz had in mind.

On the way home, she leaned forward between the seats of the F-250 supercab. "What do you think?"

"About what?" Diane asked. "You don't have your seat belt on."

Joan flopped against the back of the bench seat. "I consumed too much wine to be damaged."

"A fallacy. It's a good thing you aren't driving." Diane turned to look at her. "Which woman do you want?"

She turned her head toward the night outside the side window. Now that they were out of town, it looked very black. "I don't know. Isn't that the story of my life?"

Diane and Tania exchanged glances, and when they pulled into her driveway, Tania asked, "Are you going to be all right?"

"I always am," she said as she stumbled out of the truck. "This is not a passenger-friendly vehicle."

Diane laughed and hugged her. "Give me the keys. I'll open the door."

The next morning when she dragged herself out of bed, Yeller sat with head cocked, his tail sweeping the floor. Before work on Saturday, they usually went somewhere, either to the wetlands or for a walk or run along the roads. But it was too late to do anything but eat and shower.

At work with hair still wet, she was wiping her face and yawning away sleep when Liz walked through the door dressed in her postal shorts and shirt.

"What brings you here?" Joan asked in surprise.

"Want to go out for dinner tonight?"

"We did that last night." Yeller brushed past her, padding over to welcome Liz.

"Look, let me explain about last night. Linda just sort of invited herself along. She's my oldest friend. I couldn't say no."

"That's good, I mean, that you said yes." She wasn't used to such forthrightness from a relative stranger. "But I'm going to crash tonight. I wouldn't be good company anyway. I didn't sleep well last night for some reason." Besides, her budget only allowed one dinner out a week.

"Then why don't you come over and we'll order pizza. On me. It's my invite."

Joan looked more closely at this woman, who met her gaze frankly. She heaved a sigh.

Liz laughed. "You make me feel like a pesky gnat or something. Come on, say yes."

She caved in. "Okay. I'll come over after work. I might fall asleep on you, though."

"Hey, that's all right. I've got plenty of beds."

Then Liz was gone, leaving Joan annoyed with herself. She had wanted to go home.

Parking in front of the leaning, gray barn in the early evening, Joan slipped through the partly open door and into the cool interior. Dust motes danced in the light shafting through gaps between the warped boards. A grassy ramp led to this floor, which had been used for storing machinery. She looked up at the lofts and smelled dust from the hay and straw once stacked there. Behind the stone walls of the foundation below would be the horse stalls, the rows of stanchions, the milk and feed rooms. The building was silent except for the rustling and twittering of birds nesting in its rafters.

Yeller wagged his tail, announcing Liz's approach.

And Liz said, "I wish I could afford to save the barn."

"It's a shame to see the old buildings go. What would it cost?"

"Thousands to shore it up. It needs a new roof, new siding, paint." Liz shook her head, her hands on her hips, distress in her voice. "I have enough trouble keeping up with the house maintenance." They stepped farther inside, and the floor creaked ominously.

"I believe it," Joan said.

Liz patted her on the back, startling her. "Good to see you. Let's get out of here before the place caves in on us."

Outside in the overcast, muggy, early evening, Joan hurried to keep in step with Liz, whose strides ate up the ground. "You must spend a lot of time mowing." Although the lawn was far from looking groomed, there was a lot of it.

"Every weekend. I've thought of selling, but I feel like I'm the last surviving relative who wants the place and that I should preserve it. For what, I don't know. My nephews will probably sell it."

"Do they live nearby?"

"Nope. They're all out west." She held open the back door for Joan and Yeller.

"Not to change the subject, but who was that older couple with you at Rounders?"

"Friends of the Browns who were once friends of my folks." Liz handed her a corkscrew and a bottle of Cabernet Sauvignon. "You open that, and I'll get out some snacks."

Watching Liz pour the wine and set out crackers and cheese, Joan said, "You and Linda have a long history."

A smile broke across Liz's face, and Joan found herself staring at her mouth. It was wide with white teeth that would have been straight except for one slightly crooked eyetooth. "People are always asking me why we're not together. I was madly in love with her during our teens, all the while denying it, but I don't know if a romantic relationship can ever be forged with someone you grew up with and consider your best friend. Besides, Linda says she's bisexual."

"She was married, you said."

Liz leaned on the table before sitting down across from her. "Yes. I don't know why she kept his name. He's a jerk." She smiled resignedly. "You're interested in her, aren't you?"

Joan hesitated. "I was taken with her, till she started insulting me."

Liz laughed. "Lesbians are always coming on to her. She has to fight them off." Liz picked up a cracker and a slice of cheese. "Tell me about you."

"There's not much to tell," she said with a shrug. "What do you want to know?"

"Everything."

The fogginess of her morning brain was gone, cleared away as the dewy spider webs of early morning disappear in the sun. She told Liz, and in the telling realized again how unfocused her life had been. She had married Scott early on. Her parents liked him, he pursued her, she was fond of him, he wanted to marry her. "What kind of reasons are those anyway?" she said. She worked while he finished law school. After graduation, he offered to put her through college. She took a year of courses, but nothing caught her interest and made her want to continue. When he went to work for a law firm, they bought a house in the country. They talked about starting a family, but he gave her a horse and, instead, she began showing. That had become a passion for the remaining years of their marriage.

"And then I met Mary," she said.

"And what was that like?" Liz asked, pouring more wine.

She remembered that Yeller hadn't eaten.

Liz found a can of dog food she had put away after her dog's death. "It was a special treat. I know Yeller probably eats dry food, but it's all I've got.

"Yeller says thanks," she said, watching Liz open the can and spoon it out in a bowl next to another filled with water.

Liz said, "I thought Mary was nice enough."

"Everyone thinks she's great. She has a Teflon charm."

Liz looked at the wall clock. "We better order, and then you can tell me what you mean by that." She called in the pizza order, turned on a CD that Joan thought was George Winston, and returned to the table. "Tell me."

"Mary wasn't real. What you saw was a facade. There was no depth."

Liz looked at her intently. "What do you mean by *real*?"

Joan said, "She flatters people shamelessly, has no strong convictions about anything, and takes on the tastes of whomever she's with. She needs someone to define her."

"None of that sounds terrible."

"If she doesn't mean what she says, how do you know where you stand? She could drop you like a hot potato for the next interesting woman who came along. And she did." She laughed self-consciously. "Let's not talk about her."

* * * * *

When the pizza was gone and the crust ends fed to Yeller, it was after ten. They sat in a pool of soft, yellow light edged by darkness.

"Time to go," she said, looking across the table at Liz. "But thanks for persuading me to come."

"Why don't you stay?" Liz asked, meeting her eyes. "We can do something tomorrow."

"I've got a million things to do at home."

Liz sighed and leaned back in her chair. "So do I," she admitted.

They walked across the dewy grass to the gravel where the Bronco was parked. Joan helped Yeller onto the backseat and got in behind the wheel. She thanked Liz again and turned the key. Nothing. The battery was dead.

"I can give you a jump or you can stay," Liz said. "I think this is a sign that you should."

"I think it's a sign of my stupidity."

Liz showed her to a room across the hall from her own on the second floor, and Joan wondered how Liz could live alone in this vast house and not be scared. Besides the bed and the small table next to it that held the lamp shedding a dim glow over the room, there was a desk, a bookcase, and a large dresser. The pictures on the walls were of Liz in sports garb holding one of the many trophies that stood on the bookcase, desk, and dresser. Throw rugs littered the floor, and Yeller flopped down on one near the bed.

"This was my room when I was a kid. I didn't have to share since I was the only girl." Liz handed Joan a set of towels and washcloth, told her the bathroom was down the hall. She also gave her an extra-large T-shirt to wear to bed.

Then she was gone, and Joan turned on the desk lamp so that she could look through the books. She picked one out that she hadn't read, but had heard of, and carried it to the bed: *Curious Wine*.

After trotting to the bathroom and washing up, she opened the two windows. Leaves rustled outside, and she settled contentedly on top of the bed with the book. An hour later she was still reading.

That was when Liz knocked on her door and stuck her head through the opening. "You having trouble sleeping too?"

"I can't put the book down." She held it up.

"I couldn't either when I first read it." Liz looked softer in the dimness, younger. "Want some company?"

Joan hesitated a moment, and Liz started to pull her head out of the door opening. "Don't go," Joan said, wondering if her momentary need would mislead Liz. She didn't want her to draw the wrong conclusions. But in the end, she didn't make the decision, her desire did. "Come, sit down." She patted the bed.

Liz sat with a shy smile. "I don't know about you, but that book drove me crazy."

"I can see why," Joan said, meeting Liz's eyes boldly, letting the lust show.

Liz slid a little closer. "Do you . . . would you . . . ?"

"Yes, I want to. Right now."

"Maybe I should . . ." Liz said, getting up.

"No." Joan grabbed her wrist, pulling her off balance so that Liz fell on the bed.

Somehow they became entwined in an awkward embrace. But the kissing that followed was neither clumsy nor shy. Joan's intense passion grew out of the enforced abstinence of the past months. It exploded within her, and she rolled on top of Liz and looked down at her as if to assure herself that this was really happening. Then she kissed her nose, her eyes, her eyebrows and ears, her chin, her mouth. She traced Liz's lips with her tongue, thrust her tongue inside and was thrilled to have it pushed back in her own mouth.

They discarded their nightshirts and looked at each other. The dim light was kind, casting a shadowy glow over their bodies. Joan took a keep breath and tentatively caressed Liz's breasts. They lay heavy in her hand, the nipples large and silky. Leaning over, she buried her face in their cleavage where she breathed in the smell of Liz's skin and soap and sweat. In a single movement, she was again on top, lowering herself slowly so that their breasts and bellies met.

When they finally reached between each other's legs, they were slippery with need and came quickly under gently urgent, rhythmic strokes.

VIII

The next morning when daylight flooded the room through the tall, wavy-glassed windows, Joan at first didn't know where she was. When she remembered, she felt a stab of remorse. Unlike the dim glow cast by the bed lamp, the brightness was unkind. It bared one's skin with relentless, probing fingers.

Yeller was breathing on the back of her neck as Joan lay looking at Liz, who was very much asleep next to her. Glad that it wasn't the other way around, because she and Liz were pretty much the same age, she rose on her elbow and groped around for the

T-shirt she had abandoned with such eagerness the night before. Finding it near her feet, she dropped it over her head and shoulders.

When she turned back, she saw Liz's eyes open, squinting in the bare light. A ghost of a smile crossed her lips, an ephemeral thing that twisted Joan's heart with its hesitancy.

"Thanks," Joan said. "I mean, I needed that last night."

Liz frowned and began groping outside the sheet. Joan handed her her nightshirt, and Liz put it over her head and pulled it down modestly. "Me too. You're welcome. Come again, no pun intended."

"Hey, we both wanted it." Joan slipped out of bed and stood on the rag rug next to the bed. She looked down at it. "Did your grandma make the rugs?"

"She made that one. My mother made some, and so did I."

"They're nice." Joan met Liz's eyes, which looked a deep blue. Although she'd seen only clouds racing across the sky when she'd glanced out the window, she winced in the glare. Yeller was dancing at her feet, making a wad out of the rug. "Got to let the dog out."

"Will you be coming back?" Liz asked.

Joan hedged. "I got a lot to do today."

Liz sat up. "First we have to get your car running."

Joan had forgotten, and she let out a sigh. "It needs a new battery."

"Is it okay to have coffee and breakfast before we go to Fleet Farm and get one?" Liz looked at her watch. "Oh my god, It's only seven o'clock." She flopped back on the bed with a groan.

Joan grinned. "This is late for me and Yeller. We're usually out and about by now."

"I guess we're incompatible." Liz stood and stretched. She ran long fingers through her curls, and Joan wondered if the wave, springing away from her head and refusing to flatten, was natural. "You want to shower? I'll let the dog out and keep an eye on him."

"Sure," Joan said.

Safely under the warm spray of the shower, she felt herself being aroused by vivid memories of the night before. She was rinsing off, her head completely submerged under the cascading water, when Liz stepped into the tub with her. Joan's eyes popped open, and she saw Liz smiling, a slow twist of curling lips that gave Joan enough pause to allow it to happen again. Desire inundated her, making her as wet inside as out. They came together under the tumbling spray, slippery all over, their lips wet and warm.

Is it always better the second time, she wondered as they quickly dried each other and hurried to the bed where they'd slept. And if it's better the second time, will it continue that way? They rolled over on the crushed sheets, their legs and arms wrapped around their still damp bodies. More daring this time, they touched each other with less hesitancy, more urgency. Joan looked down the length of their joining, at their breasts fallen together, each with a leg willingly raised to grant entrance. It excited her to see their hands stroking each other, to see the other penetrate and be penetrated.

She sighed deeply.

"You all right?" Liz whispered in her ear.

In reply, Joan kissed the soft space between Liz's collarbone and neck, the warm throat and lips. They breathed into open mouths, tongues touching as orgasm engulfed first one, then the other.

Rolling away on their backs into the light of day, Joan pulled the sheet over herself and Liz did the same. They were once again shy in each other's presence.

"Do you want to finish showering?" Liz asked when the silence became uncomfortable.

"We may as well do it together," Joan said, getting up and giving Yeller a pat where he lay on the bunched-up rug. "Did he do his stuff?"

"Oh yes," Liz replied. "And took a long drink of water. I'll have to get some dog treats."

Joan had pulled the T-shirt over her nakedness again as had Liz. She pondered the implications of Liz buying dog treats for Yeller.

Over a breakfast of fried eggs, potatoes, black beans, and toast, Joan said, "I don't want you to get the wrong idea about any of this. I mean, it just sort of happened."

Liz only briefly met her eyes, and Joan thought it touchingly funny that they were having trouble looking at each other. "I know. It was nice. I hope we do it again." She smiled that hesitant smile.

"The beans are good," Joan said. "I had my doubts about beans for breakfast."

Liz laughed, the sound loud in the otherwise quiet kitchen. "I love beans."

When the phone rang, Liz got up to answer it. "Hi. What's up?" She wrapped the cord around herself, turning away from Joan, then unwound herself and said, "Can't do anything this morning, and I have to mow this afternoon. Why don't you come over later in the day?"

"Linda," Liz said, sitting down again.

"Are you going to tell her?" Joan asked.

There was the smile again, more twisted, and Joan hardened her heart to it. "No."

Joan got home around ten-thirty after she had gone with Liz to Fleet Farm and bought a new battery, which they installed in the Bronco. They had spoken little after Linda's phone call.

Next door, Lou Parry stood in the trench laying the drainage tile on its bed of stone. He was alone. The backhoe, a menacing, prehistoric-looking machine, was parked next to a diminished pile of gravel. He looked up and waved.

She went inside with the dog on her heels. Once there, she felt restless and at odds with herself. There were a million things to do: wash clothes, vacuum, cut lawn, weed flowers. Or she could go for a run or walk with Yeller, or visit Diane and Tania and ride Trixie.

She and the dog drove out to the clinic unannounced and walked through the barking, whining melee of dogs to the barn where she thought she'd find Diane and Tania. But her friends weren't there, although the truck was parked near the barn. She peered into the garage window and saw that their green Caravan was gone.

Getting Trixie out of the field, she led her into the dark aisle of the barn where the pungent smells of hay and grain enveloped them. The pony whickered from his stall and poked his small muzzle between the bars. The cats looked down at her from the lofts and meowed. Joan crosstied the horse and began cleaning her off with a currycomb and brush. Leaning over, she lifted her feet and used a hoof pick to dislodge stones and dirt. She threw her western saddle over the pad she'd laid on the horse's back and tightened the girth. Then she dropped the halter, slipped the bit between Trixie's teeth, and slid the headstall of the bridle over her ears.

Leading the horse out of the barn she opened the gate, and she and Trixie and Yeller scrabbled out through the opening into the parking lot. The dogs barked behind the gate. From the barn the pony whinnied urgently as Joan mounted and urged the horse toward the road.

They walked along the grassy berm of the road. Yeller stayed on the side of the horse away from the blacktop. Cars usually slowed before passing, but occasionally one raced by with honking horn, causing Trixie to toss her head and prance. Joan calmed the horse with steady hands and a quiet voice, even as she shook a fist at the vehicle.

"Easy, girl. They're just stupid sons of bitches."

Having trouble concentrating on her surroundings, she raised the binoculars infrequently. She heard a meadowlark, once common but now seldom seen because so many fields were mowed. She saw a pair of bobolinks, also rarely sighted for the same reason. Her thoughts kept going back to Liz, and a restlessness drove her forward without diminishing it.

Turning off the road onto a dirt lane along the edge of a field of corn, she put Trixie into a canter. The farmer who owned this land had given her permission to ride on it. The rutted road went nowhere, but it was a safe place to let the horse move. On the way back, she met Yeller halfway. He was sitting on the grass between the two lanes, waiting for her return.

They headed back toward Oakwood. When they arrived, Diane and Tania were unloading grocery bags from the van.

"Stay for supper," Diane said.

"I'm always staying for supper," Joan replied, "but I did bring some wine, just in case."

While Tania fed the animals, Joan made a salad and microwaved potatoes and Diane grilled hamburgers.

"Your friend Linda came out with her parents and got one of the puppies Saturday. Lovely people," Diane said.

A wave of disappointment swept through Joan. She had wanted to give the old couple the puppy. It had been her idea. She said nothing.

"I sense something here." Diane was looking at her. "What's going on?"

"Nothing. Well, something. I spent last night at Liz's."

Diane stopped making patties. She frowned a little, then laughed and said, "It's hard to share a best friend when you haven't had to."

"Is it? I share you," she said.

"Yeah, but you have for a long time."

"So? Does that make it easy?" She almost continued that question to its logical conclusion, telling Diane what she'd never said, that she cared for her too much.

Diane was staring at her in an unsettling way. "You never said it wasn't easy. You never suggested you weren't happy with the arrangement."

She scoffed. "How could I do that?" Tania was coming toward the house, surrounded by dogs jockeying for proximity.

"So what happened?" Diane persisted.

Joan shrugged. "We got carried away. You know how that goes."

Diane turned back to making patties. "How was it?"

"Exciting."

"It always is at first," Diane muttered as Tania came through the door.

Joan's heart pounded. She felt her conversation with Diane was a betrayal of sorts.

Tania popped the cork on the bottle of Gamay Beaujolais Joan had brought, poured three glasses, then lifted hers in a silent toast.

That night before she fell into a sleep riddled with dreams, Joan revisited the earlier conversation with Diane, dissecting each sentence. Had Diane been hinting that she too cared more than she should? It didn't matter. Diane was tied to Tania by more than love. They were in business and owned property together. And she was a friend of both. She concluded that Diane had meant exactly what she'd said and had been intimating nothing more.

Her thoughts moved on to Liz, and she squirmed as she recalled every sensation and moment of their sexual encounters. The act seemed to have reawakened a desire that she'd kept carefully under wraps long enough to have forgotten its seductive powers. Once loosed from its box, her sexual desire took on a life of its own, giving her no peace. She was better off without it.

She awakened in the night from a dream in which

she lay in the ditch with Lou Parry, who was forcing himself on her. What disturbed her was that she was halfheartedly fighting him off, worried more that he might transmit some disease he harbored than that he would have his way with her. Part of her was excited by his aggressive advances.

She got up and padded to the bathroom by the light diffused through the uncovered windows. The clouds had lifted, and the sky was littered with stars glittering through a pulsing, green atmosphere. When she was back in the bedroom, she pulled on her sweats. Yeller lifted his head from his paws.

"Come on, guy. The northern lights are putting on a show. Let's go watch."

Outside, she sprayed herself with Cutter's and dragged a cushion off a chaise longue for Yeller. Lying in the hammock, she watched the heavens throbbing in neon colors till her eyes closed and she slept. When mosquitoes stung her into wakefulness, the blush of sunrise spread across the sky.

Stiff from sleeping in the hammock, she climbed out, feeling all of her forty-nine years. "And nothing to show for it," she muttered, going inside.

At work she pondered the weekend while sweeping the floor. The order placed with Linda had been delivered, and the merchandise had to be marked and put on the shelves, which meant rearranging.

Whenever she thought of Linda, she became agitated. She reasoned she should be glad another puppy had found a home, and that the Browns had a dog in their life to take the place of the one they'd lost. Instead she felt cheated that she had only set off the chain of events and had not been invited to be a part of it.

After setting up the merchandise, she scanned the inventory on the computer and ordered replacements for what had been sold. She took a request over the phone for grain to be delivered and conveyed it to Jim in the back room.

At lunchtime she unwrapped the tuna sandwich she had brought and was putting it to her mouth when two people stepped through the door. The light was behind them, so she couldn't identify them till they moved into the interior of the store.

"Well, hi," Joan said with delight.

"Your friend Diane said you worked here during the week." Mr. Brown grinned at her.

"Don't you do anything but work, dear?" Mrs. Brown said.

A smile stretched across Joan's face, pulling the skin tight. "I was going to call you." She walked toward the door. "Is the pup with you?"

"Oh yes. Already he thinks he's a person," Mr. Brown told her.

Seeing the little dog jumping around the front seat, she asked, "Can I bring him inside?"

"Of course," Mrs. Brown said, then added, "We'd have never found him without you. You were so kind to think of us."

She turned the pup loose in the store, and he barked at Yeller, who ignored him. The puppy went wild, jumping at the big, old dog, biting his legs, growling playfully. Yeller looked down his long nose at the little creature.

"Does Linda know you're here?"

"No. We don't tell her everything," Mr. Brown said with a wink. "We have some secrets, as she does." He picked up a dog collar. "Think this'll fit Mr. Cinders?"

Joan took it from him and managed to put it around the pup's neck while he chewed on her hand. "Sure does."

The Browns bought the collar, a rawhide chip, a box of puppy treats, a bag of Purina Puppy Chow, and a leash. She walked them out to their Buick Regal and watched them drive off.

After work, she drove home where her answering machine blinked in the cool living room. There were two messages: one from David and one from Liz. David sounded desperate, and she responded to his voice by phoning him first.

"The puppy is chewing up everything in the house. At least Wolfie never did that. Guy's slippers are shredded. His mouthpiece, which cost hundreds of dollars, is unrecognizable. He doesn't touch my stuff."

She didn't know if that meant the dog was more fond of Guy or less. "Get a kennel to put him in when you're not around. We sell them at the feed mill, if you want to come buy one tomorrow."

He breathed a sigh of relief into the receiver. "I thought we were going to have to give him back. I feel like a complete failure at being a dog daddy."

"So I'll see you tomorrow?"

"I'll bring lunch," he promised.

"By the way, what did you name the dog?"

"Sylvester," he said.

Next she called Liz, but only got her answering machine. Changing clothes, she went outside to mow the lawn.

IX

When Liz called back, Joan was sitting down to a supper of Ragú sauce over spaghetti. She dragged the phone to the counter.

"I'm sorry. I phoned and then had to go outside to finish mowing the lawn, so I missed your call."

"Me too," she said, twirling pasta onto a fork.

"Look, want to go somewhere next weekend after work?"

"I can't go anywhere without Yeller." It wasn't true. She could always leave the dog at Diane's.

"We could go camping and take him with us." Liz's voice held that hesitancy that softened Joan.

She thought of all the work that went into camping. "I don't know. Do we have to decide now?"

"Well, yeah. I have to get things ready. You know, gather the camping equipment, find something to cook over the campfire."

It sounded tempting. "I have a sleeping bag, a tent, a camping stove, a cooler."

"You bring your sleeping bag. I'll take care of the rest."

Joan demurred. "That doesn't seem fair."

"It's my idea."

"Where are we going? It might be hard to find a place Saturday afternoon."

"I have a place in mind."

David showed up at noon the next day, and Joan had forgotten he was coming. He sauntered through the door, Sylvester wriggling in the crook of his arm, and she looked up from the bagel she had just unwrapped.

"I told you I was bringing lunch: leftovers from the weekend, chili verde." He set the puppy on the floor, reminding her of the Browns the day before with their pup. "I can't trust him enough to leave him at home." David sold insurance out of a small office on the access road off Highway 41.

Once again Yeller was looking down his nose at a pesky creature who nipped at his legs and barked for attention. In his excitement the pup piddled on the wood floor.

"I'll clean it up," David said when Joan brought out paper towels from behind the counter.

She showed him the kennels and put the chili verde in the microwave oven to heat. "So what else is news?" she asked when they sat down to eat the spicy food.

"Well, we're wildly happy again. Who knows how long that will last. Guy is a fickle man. He gets tired of me after a few months. As long as he keeps his affairs under wraps and is careful, I don't care. He always comes back more grateful and loving."

Looking at him as if he were crazy, she said, "How do you know he's careful?"

"Well, I am with him, so it's all right. I don't want to grow old alone."

"I'm going camping with Liz over the weekend."

"Which one is she?" he asked around a mouthful, and quickly swallowed water. "Whew. Hot stuff."

"It's good." But she too was washing it down after each bite. "She's the one without the parents. Tall as I am, curly brown hair, blue-gray eyes."

"Tell you the truth, I didn't look at either of them that well. Not the skinny one with the long hair?"

"No," she said with a sigh. "Do you think people really are bisexual?"

"She's bisexual?" he asked, and she nodded. "I suppose you have to believe what people tell you about themselves, but I always thought being bisexual was the first step toward admitting you were gay."

"Me too."

"Well, at least we know who we are. Right?" He grabbed the puppy, who was still harassing Yeller, and the kennel. "Got to go."

"You could take Sylvester to work with you."

"I'm going to, but now I can stuff him in the kennel when someone comes in. Otherwise, he bites their ankles."

The week's forecast called for hot, sunny days and warm nights. Saturday, though, was supposed to be overcast and cool. Wouldn't you know it? she thought. As soon as she planned something, the weather turned.

Saturday morning she awoke early and looked out the window at cloudy skies. A cool breeze blew in her open window and she pulled the sheet up to her chin. She lay in bed for a few moments going through a mental list of what was packed in the Bronco and what was by the front door ready for her to carry out. Yeller's cold nose prodded her cheek, and she put an arm around his neck.

At Birds of a Feather she watched the clouds piling onto each other. It had been so warm the past few weeks that this overnight cooling felt like a betrayal. She liked to sweat in summer. Yeller didn't, though, she thought, glancing at his hairy body stretched out on his rug.

Around noon, Liz came through the door in her postal garb. This time instead of shorts she wore long pants. "Just thought I'd see if you were ready to go despite the weather."

"I'll be over at your place around four." Kathy had promised to come in so that Joan could leave early.

"Good," Liz said, but she looked troubled. "Look, I've got to level with you. Linda wants to come with us. She's bringing her own tent."

Joan first felt excitement, then dismay. There would be no sex if Linda was in the next tent. Well, she decided, that was okay with her. "All right."

"You don't mind?" Liz asked with obvious relief.

"Why would I?"

Liz left, still appearing distressed.

At three-forty-five, Kathy's van screeched to a halt in front of the store. Kathy was in her late fifties, always in a hurry, and looked it. Her gray hair flew away from her head untidily. She wore a blue sweatsuit with cardinals embroidered across her ample bosom. Kathy's interests were birds, bird habitat, natural landscaping. She gave talks about how to lure birds to backyards. Opening a store like this one had been a long-time dream of hers, even though she and her husband sometimes subsidized it with other income.

"Hope I'm not late, Joan." She sounded breathless.

"You're right on time." Joan grabbed her small backpack from under the counter.

Yeller was on his feet greeting Kathy, who took his large head between her hands and cooed at him. "Sweet old dog. I hope you brought him something to lie on."

"I threw in the cushion from the chaise longue," Joan said, smiling.

"If you ever want a Saturday off, say so. And Yeller could stay with us anytime."

"I know. He could stay at Diane's too, but I have a hard time walking away from his eyes."

"Well, you go on and have fun. Hope you don't get frostbite; it's damn cold out. Supposed to get down in the high forties tonight."

"Just my luck," Joan said, going out the door.

* * * * *

Liz and Linda were loading Liz's Explorer when
Joan parked in front of the barn. She got her stuff
out of the back of the Bronco and carried it over. Liz
stood with her hands on her hips, grinning at Joan.

Linda caught sight of Liz's grin, and it was clear
to Joan that she resented it.

"Did you throw in a winter jacket?" Liz asked,
patting Yeller on the head.

"At the last minute I did. Think we're going to
freeze?"

"We don't have to go," Linda said, backing out of
the Explorer. "It'll be cold on the bay."

"If you want to stay home, I'll understand," Liz
said, and Linda looked more annoyed.

"We're going to be on the bay?" Joan asked,
assuming she meant Green Bay.

"I have a little spot there," Liz told her. "Just a
getaway."

When they got in the car to leave, Joan climbed in
the backseat. She reasoned that because Yeller was in
the back, she should be too. His nose pressed against
the window, he sat on the blanket she had thrown on
the seat to protect the upholstery. She had decided to
make a concerted effort to make Linda like her.

Linda was talking to Liz in a voice that was too
low for Joan to hear, so Joan threw an arm around
the dog and gazed out the window at the passing
scenery. Once in a while Liz would ask her a question,
but without leaning forward it was difficult to carry
on a conversation, so she answered minimally.

North of Dykesville they turned off the highway
onto a long road that led down to the bay. The road

teed into another road that paralleled the water where they turned left and drove past huge homes. When the road's surface turned to gravel, the houses dwindled to modest cottages. The road ended in an undeveloped lot where Liz parked.

They were at the top of a small rise, looking down at a rock-strewn beach and the gray waters of Green Bay. Waves crashed against the shore, splattered into shreds, and fell back into the bay, only to be covered by the next surge of water. A cold wind tugged at Joan's hair, and she pulled the hood of her sweatshirt over her head and grabbed her winter jacket out of the Explorer. The hill down to the beach was overrun with briars, among which grew bent cedars. At the top where they were parked, the lot was level and grassy with a small grove of pines, also bowed from the winter winds. Joan shivered, even in her jacket.

Liz began throwing gear out of the Explorer toward a firepit surrounded by stones. Linda placed a tarp near the pit, but the corners kept getting caught by the wind and folding over. Joan knelt and held them down.

"Thanks," Linda said, and the wind snatched her words away.

It took three of them to get the two tents upright and staked down so that they wouldn't blow away. Liz put her sleeping bag and Joan's in one tent that didn't look large enough for two people.

"You didn't bring a tent?" Linda asked, glowering at Joan.

"Liz told me not to," she said and turned to Liz for support. "Is there room for us in there, Liz?" Then she realized that even if they managed to squeeze in there, there wouldn't be room for the dog.

Linda's cheeks were a bright pink, and her long hair streamed out behind her. "You could sleep in my tent with the dog."

Without a word, Joan pulled her sleeping bag out of Liz's tent, stuffed it in Linda's and jerked Linda's out. So much for being friends, she thought.

Liz was frowning. "What are you doing?" she asked.

"She's right. There is no room for Yeller with us in there."

"Wait a minute," Liz said, and they turned toward her. "Never mind."

Liz built a windbreak for the fire out of downed limbs she gathered. Then she knelt and coaxed a flame out of the sticks they had broken and dropped in the firepit. Nursing the tiny blaze, they fed it branches until it grew enough to add the logs that were stacked under a tarp near the copse of pines nearby.

On the Coleman stove they warmed baked beans and fried steak patties. Joan had brought a bottle of Merlot. She pulled the cork and poured it into plastic glasses. Linda tore open a bag of potato chips, and they ate them before the beans were heated and the patties done. The food tasted delicious in the cold, gray evening as they sat around the fire on lawn chairs that blew away every time they stood.

Yeller had eaten the dog food Joan had brought and was lying on the chaise longue cushion at her feet. It, too, took flight whenever he got up, till she put the cooler at one end.

When Linda went off behind the stand of pines, Joan was looking around for a place to relieve herself.

She felt Liz's eyes on her from across the fire and met them.

"We still pee in the bushes," Liz said, pointing in the direction Linda had gone. "There's a trench. You just kick a little dirt in afterward."

"I see," she said, wishing she were at home where there was a bathroom and heat.

When they climbed into their respective tents, Joan took off her sweatshirt and jeans and slid down deep in the sleeping bag. Yeller lay down on his cushion next to her and leaned against her body. She could hear Liz and Linda talking in the other tent, their voices agitated. The wind flapped around the tent, lifting its corners.

She wakened sometime in the night to the sound of rain pattering on the tent. It fell softly at first, then increased in tempo until it came in sheets driven by the wind. She knew they must not touch the sides of the tent or it would leak, and she pulled the dog closer. The shelter shuddered in the wind, and the fabric soon became so drenched that it sagged inward. Before she fell asleep again, she wondered if the two women in the other tent were staying dry, but she heard nothing except the rain and wind.

Joan awakened when the sky began to lighten. The rain had stopped, but she had no desire to step outside into a cold, sodden world. The dog was awake, lying on his side with his back snug against her, his nose in the air, his tail hitting the sleeping bag. It was a full bladder that finally forced her to leave shelter.

She crawled into a diminished wind that, nevertheless, swept ragged clouds across the sky. Liz was crouched across the firepit, breathing on a little flame she sheltered with her body. Joan wondered if she looked as disheveled as Liz, whose hair stood in curly spikes on her head. They both wore the clothes they had worn to bed.

"I'm sorry I dragged you out here," Liz said. She smiled the smile that always dredged sympathy out of Joan.

Joan considered her answer. If she said she was having a great time, Liz would know it was a lie. "I needed to get away," she said, heading off toward the potty trench.

When she returned, Linda was at the fire. "My turn," she said, taking what Joan now saw was a path.

Joan got a lawn chair out of the Explorer and set it up near the fire. Patches of blue showed behind the racing clouds. The sun was high enough to offer its heat, but the wind blew cold. "And it was so hot last week," she said.

Liz smiled bleakly and nodded. She poured Joan a cup of coffee from the pot on the Coleman stove. "We have bacon and eggs and what's left of the beans for breakfast and, of course, bread."

"I'm starved," Joan said, her hand resting on Yeller's head.

Liz looked at her hard for a moment before saying, "Look, I don't know how to explain you to Linda. She wants to think of you as my friend."

"Aren't I?" Joan asked.

Liz leaned forward. "I wanted to sleep with you last night, not her." Her voice faded away as Linda walked toward them.

"It was okay," Joan said with a wry smile, looking away from the hurt on Liz's face. "Yeller kept me warm."

"What are you two talking about?" Linda said. "Boy, do I need a cup of coffee."

Liz poured another cup and handed it to her. "I'll tell you later."

"Why not now?" Linda said.

Liz stood up, her eyes suddenly blazing. She would have been impressive if her hair hadn't been so unruly and her clothes so wrinkled. "You're my best friend. Act like it."

Joan stifled the urge to laugh, although inside she was cringing, hoping this wouldn't turn into a confrontation that she would have to witness. Yeller whined deep in his throat, and she stroked his head to calm him.

Linda appeared chagrined. "I'm sorry, Liz. This is hard for me."

Liz encircled Linda's shoulders with a long arm. "Let's just fix breakfast and go home."

X

When they arrived at Liz's place, Linda transferred her gear and clothes to the Grand Am, said she had to go see her parents, and left.

Liz continued unloading the Explorer, not even looking at Joan, when she asked her to stay a while.

Joan opened her mouth to say she had to go home and do a few things, and then remembered Lou Parry. She was avoiding the house she had loved so much before he bought the lot next door. She glanced around the yard with its flourishing dandelions and patches of tall grass. "I don't want to keep you from anything."

"You won't be."

Joan threw her belongings in the Bronco and helped Liz carry things into the house. Liz dumped everything at the foot of the stairs. In the kitchen, she put water on to heat. Then she went in the living room and started a fire in the fireplace.

Joan had never been in the living room and followed her there. The old house was damp. Liz had turned a light on, and Joan sat on the edge of the couch under it, watching the fire take hold. The smell and sight of burning wood warmed her.

Liz swiveled on her heels. "Stay there." She was back in a few minutes with hot chocolate. "God, I don't think I'm ever going to be warm again," she said, handing Joan a mug.

Cupping her hands around the warmth, Joan stared at the fire. Yeller, too, sat with eyes riveted on the flames. "Thanks. A little heat feels good inside and out."

Liz sat down next to her. "I'm so sorry about the weekend."

She turned and studied the shadows of Liz's face. "Hey, it was okay. Something to do. An escape from Lou Parry and his backhoe."

"I thought it would be fun, and it turned into something like a nightmare."

"It's not your fault the weather was rotten."

But Liz wouldn't let it go. "It's my fault Linda came with us."

If she hadn't looked so dejected, Joan would have told her not to beat a dead horse. Instead, she patted her on the knee. "Linda doesn't like me, does she?"

"It's not you. We've been friends so long she thinks I belong to her."

"You've been with other women, haven't you?" Joan asked.

"I was with someone last summer when we played volleyball. Our relationship was going to pot about the same time yours with Mary must have been doing the same." Liz heaved a sigh. "I should get a dog."

Joan laughed. "What the hell does a dog have to do with anything?" She looked around. "Where's the cat?"

"Hiding." Liz gave her a slightly bemused look. "A dog is loyal, affectionate, kind. Look at Yeller there."

Yeller had moved closer to the fire and now lay on the hearth rug. He responded to his name by lifting his head.

"Well, we could call Diane. There's one puppy left."

"Not now," Liz said. "I'd want to take him home on a Saturday so he could get used to the place before I have to leave for work."

"Good thinking. Do you want me to call, though, and ask Diane to hang on to him?"

"Sure."

When she hung up, she said, "You're in luck. The puppy's still there. They took him into the house because he was lonely."

Liz leaned forward on the couch, her hands hanging between her legs, her eyes dark in the meager light. She cleared her throat. "Are you hungry?"

Joan was. She glanced around the room at the tall ceilings and dark woodwork, at the wallpaper that had a small busy pattern she couldn't see well enough to identify. "For popcorn."

They ate it in front of the fire. Yeller always lost

his manners when there was popcorn. He watched alertly as each piece disappeared into their mouths. They tossed him bits and he caught them midair.

After the popcorn was gone, Liz put another log on the fire. The room was getting warm, and Joan took off her sweatshirt. She felt sleepy.

She awoke to find herself on her side facing the back of the couch, her own breath bathing her face. Aware of voices behind her, she turned over on her back. She was covered with an afghan. Yeller put a dry nose on her cheek and licked her.

Placing a hand on the dog's head, she buried her fingers in his ruff. Sluggish with sleep, she turned so that she was facing the dog. Embers pulsed in the fireplace. She could see Liz in the kitchen. Swinging her legs over the edge of the couch, she sat up and ran her fingers through her hair.

When she walked through the darkened dining room to the brightly lit kitchen, she realized that the voices came from the radio. Liz was chopping vegetables at the butcher block table. "Stir fry. I'm using up all the leftovers in the fridge."

A bottle of wine stood open on the counter with two glasses next to it. Outside, clouds were still playing peekaboo with the sun. A thermometer fastened to a tree read fifty-five degrees. The windowpanes rattled in their frames.

"What happened to summer?" she said.

"This won't last," Liz assured her.

"Why didn't you wake me?" She stood watching Liz chop.

"Why would I? You looked so peaceful."

"Can I help?" she asked.

"You can talk to me."

Joan leaned against the table. "It's time for me to entertain you. Why don't you come over for dinner next Saturday night?"

Liz glanced up and smiled, erasing some creases and creating others. Her fingers were long and blunt, her hands broad. They looked capable. "Love to. Maybe you could go with me first to pick up the puppy."

"Sure."

"I bought some dog food for Yeller when he's here," Liz said. "It's under the sink. Is it time for him to eat?"

Having food for Yeller on hand was thoughtful, yet it was an assumption. Joan thanked Liz and fed the dog. "If Yeller doesn't finish it off, the puppy can when he grows up."

They ate the stir fry, which had bits of broccoli, carrots, onions, chicken, and pork sautéed in olive oil and sprinkled with soy sauce, with rice and bread that Liz's breadmaker had produced.

It was still light when they finished cleaning up the dishes and putting away the uneaten food. Joan needed to go home. There were things to do before she went to work tomorrow, like run a couple of loads of wash and iron some clothes.

"Will I talk to you during the week?" Liz asked, shivering in her lightweight jacket.

"Give me a call," Joan said, unrolling the window of the Bronco a few inches. "And thanks for everything."

Liz stepped back and raised a hand as she turned the Ford around and drove off.

The evening was cold and unfriendly. She attributed the weather to the absence of Lou Parry and the backhoe. He had been working late during the long days in the hot weather.

She and Yeller went inside. The house was chilly and lonesome. She thought of building a fire, but decided there was no time to sit around and enjoy it. Gathering up her dirty clothes, she took them to the basement. While they washed, she put away the camping equipment she had taken with her that weekend.

She fell in bed around ten, and Diane called. Joan told her about the weekend, and they howled with laughter over the sleeping arrangements and the weather.

Although the bed felt luxuriously soft and warm after the night on a pad on the uneven ground with rain lashing the tent, she tossed restlessly for what seemed hours. Outside, the wind still blew. The shadows of trees bent on her bedroom walls. Jumping out of bed, she went to the window and spotted a dusk-to-dawn light on Lou Parry's lot.

Her anger spurred her to pull on sweats and cross the yard to the muddy expanse next door. The light was wired to an electrical line that ended at the pole. She banged on the pole with her fists till she became conscious of Yeller at her side, looking up at her with alarm.

"Goddamn him, Yeller. There he goes turning the night into day." She had loved the dark, quiet nights.

Searching the ground for rocks, she threw them at the light. When they hit, they made a chinking sound before falling back to the ground without doing any damage. Her arm ached before she finally hit the light with enough power to shatter it. Then she stood stock-still, shocked at her first act of vandalism.

In bed, she pondered whether preserving what she valued was vandalism. She didn't want the night lit with artificial light. Why should it be forced on her? Finally, she slept.

The next morning she was exhausted. She dressed in jeans and a long-sleeve shirt and drove to work in a daze. Water thundered over the dam next to the feed mill, and cedar waxwings snatched insects out of the misty spray. Their keening reached her ears.

Inside, the building smelled dusty and sweet. She sneezed. Turning on the computer, she got the start-up money out of the change box hidden behind some books, counted it, and put it in the cash register. At the end of the day, Jim Taggart would take all but the start-up amount and deposit it.

She read the note Jim had left for her on the desk. Someone was coming in for two tons of horse feed at eight-thirty. The bags were stacked by the door. Jim was gone, delivering another order.

An arrogant young man showed up with an F-350 truck, a fancy crew cab with dual rear axles that the horse people called a dually, at nine A.M. to pick up the feed. She helped him carry out the fifty-pound bags. Wind swept around the corner of the building, bringing moisture from the stream. Two large Rottweilers were ranging around the parking lot and came running when they saw Yeller standing on the porch.

"Those your dogs?" Joan asked, dropping the bag in the bed of the truck.

"Yeah," he said.

"Do you mind putting them back in the truck?"

"They ain't doing nothing," he grunted, spitting off to one side and dropping another bag on top of the ones already in the bed. A round can of snuff was visible in the rear pocket of his jeans.

Yeller alertly jumped to face one dog and then the other when they sniffed at him. They made her nervous because they were obviously making him. One dog lunged at him, and Yeller snarled. The other bit him from behind, and Yeller yelped.

"Put them away or I'll shoot them," she said, running toward the dogs. Jim kept his rifle and shotgun in the office locked up in a case, but she had never shot anything.

The man opened the truck door and called the dogs. They ignored him. She grabbed one by the collar, and it turned and bit her. Shock waves ran up her arm. The young man no longer looked arrogant. He leaped onto the porch, took hold of both dogs, and dragged them to the truck. Then he returned, obviously worried.

"Are you all right?"

There was blood on Yeller's coat and Joan's arm. "Neither one of us is all right," she said.

"They never done nothing like that before."

"You shouldn't let them run loose." She was furious.

"You let *him* run loose," he said, indicating Yeller.

"He belongs here, and he doesn't bite," she snapped. "Have they had their rabies shots?"

He nodded. "Yes. I'm sorry."

"You'll be getting the bills."

When he was gone, she went inside with Yeller and parted his coat to see how badly he was hurt. Using a wet paper towel, she dabbed at the torn skin. Her arm had stopped bleeding. The dog had sunk its teeth, creating two puncture wounds. She knew she would have to be seen by a doctor. Her arm throbbed already.

When Jim got back, she took Yeller to Diane's, left him there, and drove herself to Immediate Care. She refused to let either Diane or Tania go with her. At the clinic the doctor cleansed the red-rimmed bites and gave her a shot and a sampling of antibiotics.

She drove back to work and called Diane. It was noon. Diane told her Yeller was fine; they'd shaved off a patch of hair and stitched him together. Joan said that she was okay and that she'd pick him up after work.

After hanging up, she sat for a while. She felt strange. Her head buzzed and her arm throbbed. She didn't hear Diane come in, didn't know anyone was there, till Diane spoke.

"You look like shit. Did you really go to the doctor?"

She looked up and thought she was imagining her. It seemed as if Diane had materialized out of nowhere. She shook her head. The room moved and wavered.

"Yes. I went to my vet." She laughed at the pale joke.

"I think you better go back," Diane said.

But Joan couldn't get out of the chair.

Diane disappeared and reappeared with Jim. They both stared at her for a moment. Diane put a hand to her forehead, but she knew she didn't have a fever because she was covered with cold sweat.

"I'm going to take her to Immediate Care."

The two of them helped her out of the chair. Her ears rang and sweat popped out all over her. It was hard to form words. "Just there," she said.

"I think she's having a reaction to whatever they gave her," Jim remarked.

"Be fine," she tried to say.

They bundled her into Diane's truck with Yeller in the back. The dog licked her cheek.

"Why did you come?" she asked, but the words ran together.

"I don't know. I was worried. You sounded funny on the phone."

The doctor gave her an antidote, and with Diane by her side she lay for an hour on a gurney till she was allowed to go home. Twice Diane went outside to check on Yeller. Fortunately, the day was cool and the open windows let in enough air.

"You're coming home with me," Diane said. "We'll pick up some of your things first."

She felt like a person recovering from a serious illness: elated yet weak, ready to take on the world in two-minute rounds. "I should go back to work."

"No way," Diane said.

At Joan's house Diane gathered clothes together and filled a bag with personal necessities as Joan shuffled behind her, still a little dazed and off center.

In the guest bedroom at Diane and Tania's she fell on the double bed and closed her eyes to the afternoon. Yeller dropped to the rug by her side with a thump and a sigh. Her dreams were violent. In them barking dogs surrounded her and Yeller on three sides, alternately attacking and retreating. She and Yeller were backed up against a fence, facing the animals. Her arm ached from holding a stick that she used as a weapon. When one of the snarling canines snapped it in two, she awakened to darkness. Yeller was on his feet, greeting her with his version of a tap dance.

Remembering the dizziness, she got up slowly and made her way to the living room where there were lights and voices. A small, black furry dog assaulted her ankles. His teeth clamped onto her jeans and she dragged him across the floor for a few steps till he saw Yeller and let go to torment him instead.

Diane and Tania put down the magazines they were reading and greeted her with concern.

"I'm okay," she assured them.

"I'll go heat up leftovers," Tania said.

And she became aware of the emptiness of her stomach, a hollowness around which she remained upright.

XI

The week vanished as day by day she was kept busy with customers. When she went home at night, she checked to see if the dusk-to-dawn light was still broken. The throbbing in her arm lessened each day, and the angry redness surrounding the puncture wounds faded to pink. She told Diane to send a vet bill to the farm that owned the Rottweilers.

Friday after work she took Yeller home and drove to the huge grocery store where she shopped. She bought a salmon filet, lemons, a bottle of Chardonnay, wild rice, salad makings, and her usual groceries to get her through the week.

Wheeling her cart into a checkout aisle, she found she was right behind the Browns and their daughter, Linda. Delighted to see the older couple, she asked about Mr. Cinders.

"You'll have to come visit. He keeps us laughing," Mrs. Brown said.

"I will one of these days, but I'll call first." She wondered if she ever would, now that she knew Linda was not in the picture.

Linda asked, "What happened to your arm?"

Joan looked down at the bandage almost with surprise. She'd nearly forgotten it was there without the constant throb to remind her. "Dog bite."

"Not Yeller," Mrs. Brown exclaimed.

"Yeller got bit, too. A couple of Rottweilers." They would have eaten Mr. Cinders.

"Is Yeller all right?" Mrs. Brown looked genuinely concerned.

"Yeah, he's okay." She smiled.

"You take care of yourself, honey," Mr. Brown said when their groceries were bagged, "and come see us."

When she got home, Lou Parry was standing under the broken dusk-to-dawn light staring up at it. His jeans hung on his hips. He walked over to the Bronco and asked if she knew what had happened.

She cleared her throat. She'd had days to think about what she'd say to him at this moment, and she was coming up blank. "Why move to the country if you don't like the dark or the woods or the birds and other wildlife?"

"What?" he said, frowning. "You broke the light?"

"You put up another one and I'll break it too." She took a deep breath and stood her ground.

He chewed on his lip as he thought. "People are more comfortable stealing materials in the dark."

"You can store them in my garage if you don't put up another dusk-to-dawn light," she said. She seldom put the Bronco under cover.

"Deal," he said, holding out his hand for her to shake. His teeth had gaps between them, but they were straight and white. "I'll help you with the bags."

"That's okay," she said, her hand in the grip of his hairy one. His boots were muddy.

He carried the bags to the door of the kitchen where she took them from him. "Want a margarita?" he asked. "I've got a cooler full of them little bottles. Ice cold. A lady I did some work for today gave them to me."

"As soon as I put the groceries away, I'll come out."

They sat in lawn chairs in her backyard and drank. She pointed out the bluebirds nesting in the boxes on top of the posts near the woods. She showed him the bat house and told him how they ate thousands, no millions, of mosquitoes.

"You're one of them nature persons, aren't you?" he said after the second margarita had gone down.

"I am. Even dead trees serve a purpose. The insects in them feed birds, and they provide homes for wildlife."

"I suppose you're mad because I cut them trees down," he said, mellowing even more after a third margarita.

"Not mad. Sad," she said, mellowing out herself. "I

bought this house to get away from traffic and lights and people."

"I'm building this house to make a buck." He laughed loudly.

They craned to see when a vehicle drove into her driveway, and Yeller got up to investigate. She thought it was probably Diane, making sure she was all right. Instead, David walked around the side of the house, the new puppy in his arms. He looked distraught.

"David! What's up?" She started to get out of her chair, only then realizing that the margaritas packed a wallop.

"Diane told me what happened to you and Yeller Monday. I said I'd check up on you."

Joan introduced David to Lou and they shook hands. Lou reached into the cooler and pulled out a bottle. "Have a margarita," he said with a grin. His wispy hair floated around his head.

"Thanks," David said, taking it from him and sitting down in an empty lawn chair. "You don't mind if I join you?"

Lou waved a hand through the air. "Why not?" He pointed at his broken dusk-to-dawn light. "She did that. Put a rock through it." He sounded impressed.

"You did?" David asked, looking at her.

"It was lighting up my bedroom," she said, and Lou laughed as if it was the funniest thing he'd heard.

David set the wriggling puppy on the ground, where he immediately launched himself at Yeller.

By the time the sun slipped out of sight and the evening chill forced them into jackets, they were howling like fools. Everything anyone said made them collapse with laughter. Convulsed with mirth, Lou's small, sturdy, hairy body rolled into a ball, his face lit with a twisted hilarity.

David rocked back and forth, clutching his midriff, hawing loudly into the night. He slapped at mosquitoes and laughed harder, stomping the ground with his feet.

Joan roared with them, even as she wondered what they were finding so amusing. They looked funny. Maybe that was it. Her stomach, abdominal, and facial muscles ached, proving that too much laughter was painful.

Yeller's eyes flicked from one to the other, his head cocked, patient with the puppy that chewed on his jowls. Occasionally he growled a warning, which went unheeded. Sylvester hung from his lip, and everyone laughed as Joan gently pried the puppy's teeth apart and handed him to David.

"I'll take him home," David said, struggling to his feet and swaying.

She said, "No one's going anywhere before we eat."

She made them take off their shoes before she retrieved the salmon from the fridge, seasoned it, and put it under the broiler while she baked potatoes in the microwave oven and fixed a salad. They ate hungrily, but they were no more sober than before they started.

So she told them they couldn't drive, showed them the spare bedrooms in the loft, and gave them towels. Then she went to bed and passed out.

Early in the morning Lou was next door, tromping around his lot. Joan called to him when she took the puppy outside, and he came over. David was still asleep. Sylvester had spent the night in a box in the kitchen.

She fixed toast. David came yawning and stretching from the bedroom at the top of the stairs. She could hardly believe last night had happened. The three of them seemed so unalike.

David said, "Thanks, Joanie, for everything. I was miserable as sin when I came over. You never would have guessed it, would you?"

"I have to go to work and then to the store. We ate tonight's dinner."

Lou fished in his pockets and plopped a ten on the table, and she shook her head. "You brought the drinks."

Not to be outdone, David put a ten on top of Lou's. "I brought nothing but trouble there." He nodded at Sylvester, who was yipping at Yeller as the old dog held him down with a large paw.

When she left for work, David was helping Lou stack bags of cement in her garage.

"Who's coming over?" David asked. Sweat dribbled down his face, and he wiped it off with the back of his gloved hand.

"Liz," she said.

"Ah." He smiled sadly. "Guy left me, and I told him not to come back."

"I'm sorry," she said, thinking maybe it was a good thing since Guy was far from faithful.

"Me too. I don't know what got into me." He sighed.

She helped Yeller into the Bronco. "Good sense, maybe."

The Case growled to life next door, and Lou drove it over with its front end loader full of bags of cement.

The day was warm, the sun hot on the side of her

face and the arm that hung out the window. Glad to have the summer back, she hummed along to a *Carmen* suite by Bizet on public radio.

After work, she purchased New York steaks and a bottle of Cabernet. She would marinate the steaks, bake a couple of potatoes, fix another salad, and make some bread in her breadmaker.

When she got home David and Lou were gone. She fixed the marinade and lay down for a few minutes. The smells of pines and columbine and sweet clover floated through the windows on a soft breeze that brushed her skin. She fell asleep to the sounds of birds: doves cooing in the lilac bush outside her window, blue jays screeching in the woods, crows cawing in the distance, bluebirds singing in the backyard.

The doorbell woke her up. Smoothing her hair into a semblance of order, she went to answer it. Liz stood outside the screen.

Liz gave her a bottle of Merlot. "I took a guess, not knowing what was for dinner."

"Good guess," she said.

"Are you ready to get the puppy?"

She had forgotten about the puppy in the foolishness of last night and the events of the day. "Oh sure. Let me brush my hair and we'll be on our way."

"What happened to your arm?"

"Dog bite. Look at Yeller's back. He got bit too."

They took the Bronco, and Joan told Liz of the previous night's hilarity. "I guess we were bombed out of our minds. I was sleeping when you got here."

"I thought so."

Diane was waiting for them when they got to the clinic. After looking at Yeller's shaved, stitched wound, she insisted on seeing Joan's.

Joan had been very careful about the bandage, but it had been hard to keep it clean, so Diane replaced it with a new one after she took a peek at the puncture wounds.

Diane knew the people at the farm that owned the Rottweilers. "They've got money and nice horses," she said. "They sent me a check for stitching up Yeller and they asked after you. I hope this makes them start penning up those dogs."

Tania brought the pup out and handed him to Liz. "If you change your mind, bring him back. We fell in love with him."

The other dogs milled around the gate, looking for a pat. Joan reached between the bars and scratched their ears. They sat on their haunches and panted, occasionally licking her hand. Wolfie was rangier, calmer.

"What are you going to name the puppy?" Diane asked.

"Black Buddy," Liz replied as the little dog tried to climb out of her arms.

"Poor Yeller must think there is no end to these look-alike puppies," Joan said as they climbed back in the Bronco. "See you guys."

Joan grilled the steaks on the gas grill on the brick patio outside the sliding glass doors off the kitchen. She microwaved the potatoes, and Liz cut up vegetables while she tore apart the lettuce for a salad.

They ate on the small round glass-top table on the

patio. "We were supposed to be feasting on salmon. That's what I initially bought for our dinner. We ate it last night."

Liz laughed.

After dinner, they sat in the backyard as darkness fell slowly and subtly.

Liz said, her head back, "Look at those trillions of stars."

But Joan was feeling an unexpected stirring of desire. Overhead, diamonds glittered against a velvety black sky. But she wondered not at their beauty; she wondered how she could initiate something that would lead to sex. She remembered that Liz had not made a sexual move last weekend and wondered why. Perhaps she was no longer interested in her that way.

"Want to go inside?" Joan asked.

"Sure, if you want to." Liz sounded surprised.

The rooms seemed too bright, and Joan began to load the dishes in the dishwasher.

Liz handed her the plates, glasses, and flatware stacked in the sink. "Did I do something wrong?"

"No. It's me."

"What is it?"

Joan straightened and looked Liz in the eye. "Why didn't you want me last Sunday?"

Liz stared at her for a few moments. "I'd screwed up the weekend. I was afraid I'd scare you away."

"Come on," Joan said, taking Liz's hand.

After dropping their clothes on the floor, Joan threw off the covers and pulled Liz into bed with her. Only when she was looking up into the dark blue of Liz's eyes did she ask herself what the hell she was doing. She hardly knew this woman, but she liked her and she loved her body. Liz was an athlete gone to seed. There was a core of hardness to her, but it was covered by softer, fuller flesh.

She tried to ignore the puppy, whining and jumping at the bed. This puppy seemed more interested in people than other dogs, which for Yeller must have been a relief. They should have put him in a box.

Just as she was getting lost in the kissing, and her excitement was spinning out of control, the phone rang. Both of them jumped.

"Let it ring," Joan said.

The sound echoed through the quiet house, punctuated by the puppy's yips. On the fourth ring, the answering machine clicked on and after the beep, Linda said, "Liz, if you're there, pick up the phone." When no one did, she hung up and the dial tone buzzed in the void.

It threw water on their passion, and Joan said, "There's something here you haven't told me."

"There's nothing. Can we start over?" Liz asked.

"We can try."

XII

Joan awakened as sunshine filtered into the room. It lit Liz's features on the pillow next to her own, and she studied them for a few seconds. Liz's eyes moved under her lids, her mouth worked a little, she scratched her nose, but her breathing continued soft and steady.

Then she heard the diesel engine of the Case growling next door and knew that it had roused her. Carefully getting out of bed, she started to tiptoe out of the room, gathering her clothes off the floor as she went.

"I'll take him out. He's my responsibility." Liz's throaty voice stopped her.

"That's okay. I'll do it." She turned, saw Liz up on one elbow.

"Promise to hurry back?" Liz flopped back and pulled the sheet over her head.

"Yeah. Stay there."

Fearing that the pup would pee on the kitchen floor, she carried his box outside and released him there. Lou waved from his perch on the backhoe and she waved back. Buddy barked at the machine, and Yeller went to the edge of the yard to do his business. Unlike last Sunday, the morning air was summer soft.

After starting the coffee, she returned to the bedroom. Liz was lying on her side, her breasts nestled one on top of the other. Joan slid her fingers between them to separate and define them. Opening her eyes, Liz pulled her down so that they lay with legs and arms entwined, bellies and breasts and lips touching.

Later, when they got up and showered and ate breakfast, Joan remembered the softness of their bodies together and felt the lust welling up. But the phone rang and she answered it.

"Hi, Linda." She met Liz's eyes and mouthed the words *Are you here?* Liz nodded, and she handed her the receiver.

"We, um, were busy. Why did you call?" Liz's hair hung in wet curls. She wore the slacks and shirt she'd had on the day before. "I don't know. I'll phone you when I get home." She hung up and met Joan's eyes.

"Why did she call last night?" Joan asked.

"No reason. She wanted to talk."

"She acts like a jealous lover," Joan said.

Liz nodded. "I know, but she's never been my

lover, not even when I wanted her to be." She jerked her head toward the lot next door. "That's Lou out there?"

"Yep. Tearing up his piece of the world."

"What are you going to do today?" Liz asked.

"Haven't decided yet whether it's to be the wetlands or Diane's or a walk down the road."

"Can I do it with you?" Liz said, her eyes cobalt blue in the light of day.

In the latter part of the afternoon Liz went home to mow her lawn, Lou loaded up the backhoe and drove away, and Joan was left alone with Yeller. A natural silence descended on her small plot of land, and she decided to clear a way to the creek. Spraying herself and Yeller with mosquito repellent, she climbed over Lou's bags of cement in the garage to retrieve the machete. Nearing the creek, her way blocked by sumac and tangles of blackberry bushes, she hacked away at the interlacing branches and the vines that clung to her jeans.

Sweat ran into her eyes, and mosquitoes and deerflies lit on her. She nearly drove the blade into her shoulder, swatting at the insects. When she reached the creek, she heard the sweet song of a brown thrasher and saw warblers flitting from bush to bush. The stream was only two feet wide there with grassy embankments and patches of poison ivy. Looking into the brown, curling water, wondering if it was deep enough to harbor trout, she stepped off the edge into the icy stream.

The water covered her boots and jeans halfway up to her knees, plenty deep enough for fish. Something bumped her leg and moved on, and she saw it was a water snake. A deerfly stung her on the neck, and she jumped out of the water and slogged her way back to the yard where Yeller waited.

"You sissy," she chided him, and he wagged his tail slowly but made no move to get up.

Spraying herself again, she put on a ball cap and plunged back into the trees. The woods were a mix of oaks and pines till she got to the sumac. With gloved hands, she dragged the branches and vines she'd chopped and piled them near the edge of her backyard. The cap deterred the flies from buzzing her head, and frequent spraying kept the insects off her skin. When she finished, she had a respectable pathway to the stream. Tomorrow after work she would put a worm in the water and see if she could entice any- thing to bite.

Monday dawned cloudy and cooler after a night of rumbling thunder and lightning danced on the horizon as she drove to work. She unlocked the front door at the mill and entered the cool, quiet building with Yeller at her heels.

Midmorning as she stacked shelves, the rain began falling. At first it pattered on the roof, then it fell so hard the droplets leaped off the pavement in a mist. While she worked, she thought about what she liked best about Liz and concluded that it was her unassuming ways.

When the door opened and Linda came through it, water coursing off her umbrella, Joan looked at her with surprise.

"What brings you here?"

"You," Linda said. She wore toffee-colored slacks and a white blouse that clung to her breasts.

"Me?" Joan said stupidly.

"Yes, you," Linda replied with a slight smile. "I'm inviting you to dinner at my place tonight."

"Is Liz going to be there?" Joan asked, unable to make sense of this. But Linda looked lovely with her hair twisted over her shoulders and her eyes so clear of guile, it would be easy to forgive her past transgressions.

"No." Linda sounded annoyed. "I bought a tenderloin. Does that tempt you?"

"You don't even like me," she said.

Linda's smile deepened so that she looked genuinely amused. "Yes, I do."

"What time?" she asked, surprising herself.

"Six-thirty. Bring the dog if you like."

Joan glanced down at Yeller, and when she looked up the door was closing and Linda was running under the umbrella to her car. Joan's heart thrummed in her ears, and she was useless the rest of the day. She'd be doing something and find herself forgetting to finish, staring out the windows at the rain.

She knocked on Linda's door with a bottle of wine in hand. She hoped not but she thought it might be the same Merlot Liz had given her. After work, she had gone home and showered and tried on at least five different pairs of slacks and blouses, discarding all but one outfit in a heap on the bed.

David had phoned. He was the only person she had told of her plans tonight. "You're playing with fire," he'd said. "She could be doing this to use it against you with Liz."

"What do you mean?" she'd asked, knowing full well what he meant.

"Why else would she suddenly ask you over?" he'd said. "You yourself said she detested you."

"Because she changed her mind and wants to get to know me?" But she'd doubted the truth of that.

Her heart still thrummed in her throat and knocked noisily in her chest. She had been unable to turn Linda's invitation down because she'd wanted her from the first time she saw her. Liz was nice, but Linda was galvanizing.

You're not nice, she told herself, but she already knew that. Taking a deep breath, she placed a hand on Yeller's head and waited for the door to open.

Linda wore wide-leg satin shorts and a short-sleeve, V-neck blouse of the same material. A gap between the shorts and the top revealed a flat midriff. There was no sagging flesh in sight.

"Have any trouble finding the place?" Linda asked as Joan stepped into her living room.

"Nope." She didn't admit to locating the house weeks ago. Looking around she saw an ordinary interior, rather spartan in furnishings. The walls were off white, the furniture modern. Lots of green plants flourished in the windows.

Joan followed Linda into the kitchen and sat at a counter on a high stool. Two glasses of wine and a plate of cheese and crackers awaited them. Joan took a wineglass and glanced around at the efficiently arranged work space. In an alcove encircled by windows a table was set for two. Wonderful smells came from the oven.

"How'd you have time for this?" she asked.

"I set things up on Sunday." Close up, Linda's

thick hair was laced with gray, coiling around her shoulders in large waves. Her smile was wonderful: teeth straight, lips full.

"How are your folks?" Joan said, trying to keep herself from saying something embarrassingly flattering.

A trace of a frown appeared. "Good. They love the puppy."

"I thought they might," she said. "You don't like me to ask after them?"

"Why would I mind?" Linda said, but Joan felt she did.

Linda removed the stuffed tenderloin from the oven, sliced it, and put it on the table with potatoes, gravy and a salad.

The food melted in Joan's mouth, and she couldn't say enough good things about dinner. But she was suddenly so self-conscious that she actually ate very little. "I didn't know you were a gourmet cook."

Linda said, "For all that praise, you're not eating much."

"I know. I'm nervous. I don't know why I'm here." She blushed and looked away.

"You're here because I asked you."

"I don't know why you did," she said honestly.

Linda put down her fork and knife. "Look, you're right. I thought you were kind of intrusive at first. But if Liz thinks you're okay, then you are." She shrugged her shoulders, and the material slid over her breasts.

"I liked you from the first," Joan said.

"Good. Now eat something."

For dessert Linda had made a butterscotch flan. But by then Joan was so tense with all that was unsaid her stomach hurt when she put anything in it.

She helped clear the table and load the dishwasher after dinner, then followed Linda back to the living room, where she said, "I better go soon. I have to get up early."

"Sit with me for a while," Linda said, patting the leather couch.

Nervously, Joan tried to come up with a tactful reason to leave. She was not up to a seduction, no matter who contrived it. "Tell me about yourself," she said.

"What do you want to know?" Linda asked.

"I know you're a golfer, that you were married, that you've been friends with Liz for years, that you sell animal products, that your parents are sweet people."

"You know more than I know about you then." Linda's brown eyes met hers squarely. Joan looked into their depths and knew why she was here.

They did it on the couch with their clothes on. It was hurried, hands-in-the-pants sex, the kind Joan had experienced in high school with boys. When they were done, she went into the half bath off the living room and washed her hands. She felt terrible and wondered if Linda did too.

"Now I do have to go," she stammered when Linda returned from the bathroom down a hallway. "Thanks for a wonderful dinner and a nice evening."

Linda looked rumpled and sexy. "Do you feel guilty?"

"Yes. Don't you?"

She nodded. "Liz is my best friend. With friends like me who needs enemies?" Her smile was wry.

"I hate to come and go — or come and come," Joan said, unable to resist the pun. She had climaxed, quick and hard. "See you soon." And she and Yeller went out the door into the rainy night.

At home there was a message from Liz on her machine. "Give me a call when you get back."

Instead, she went to bed and escaped into sleep.

After work the next day, Joan made her way to the stream with her rod and a container of worms in hand. Threading a worm on a hook, she flipped the line in the creek as the brown thrasher sang its evening song and the warblers flitted through the bushes. Stepping into the cool water in her high boots, the brim of her cap pulled down over her eyes, she flicked the line as the worm sank in the stream. When a trout hit unexpectedly, rising from under the embankment and taking the bait, she remembered the forgotten thrill. Reeling the fish in, she released it without ever taking it out of the water.

As she worked her way downstream, the sun fell lower in the sky, its slanting rays barely penetrating the woods. The deerflies and mosquitoes bit fiercely after the rain. Slogging her way upstream to where she had started, she walked out of the woods to where Yeller waited in the backyard.

Inside, she fed the dog and fixed herself a grilled cheese sandwich and baked beans for supper. Remembering how little she'd eaten the previous night, she was mentally kicking herself when the phone rang.

"You didn't return my call last night," Liz said.

"I got home too late." Her heart pinged guiltily.

Liz was silent for a moment. "I heard you had dinner at Linda's."

"Did you?" she said, instantly annoyed. She was still a free agent, wasn't she?

"She's a good cook," Liz said after another small silence.

"I didn't think she liked me."

"Why wouldn't she?" Liz asked.

It came to her that this was a cat-and-mouse conversation, just like the one last night. "Because you liked me."

Liz sounded downcast. "She's my friend."

"Is she?" Joan couldn't help asking.

"Want to go out for fish Friday night?" Liz asked.

"Sure. I'll pick you up. I have to go home and drop Yeller off first."

The week passed without her hearing from Linda. Diane called and asked her to come out on Sunday. Joan said she'd bring dinner. David phoned Thursday night.

"How was your date with Linda?"

"Weird. I don't think I've ever been so uncomfortable, but she's a great cook."

"Anything happen?"

She hedged. "I'm not sure."

"What the hell does that mean?"

"I don't want to talk about it. What happened last Saturday with Lou?"

"He let me work the backhoe and drive the tractor. It was great fun."

"And Guy?"

"Who knows? Look, you want to go out for fish tomorrow night?"

"I've already been asked by Liz."

"Maybe I could meet you two at Diversity. I won't horn in."

"I'm not sure there's anything to horn in on. Linda told Liz I had dinner at her house."

"See, I warned you."

"I hate people who say I told you so."

When she hung up, night was coming on. July had turned into August, and the days were noticeably shorter. Crickets chirred loudly. Something screamed once, causing Yeller to raise his head and prick his ears. She jumped, her scalp shivering. Going to the patio door in the darkened kitchen, she saw nothing.

"Probably a rabbit," she said to the dog, whose tail swept the floor.

The house was quiet with only the refrigerator humming and the wall clock ticking. She put Saint-Saën's organ symphony on the CD player and sat down with the newspaper. This third symphony was so haunting that she let the paper fall in her lap after reading a few words. An unnamed sadness welled up, and she found herself wallowing in remorse. She would turn fifty in September. She had no sisters or brothers, no kids, only a few real friends, no accomplishments. Who would write her obituary? Diane? And what would she say outside of date of birth and death, parents, no survivors, place of work, interests? Who would come to the funeral if she died tomorrow?

She felt tears on her face and wiped them away with the heels of her hands. Yeller got up and laid his head in her lap, and she laughed a little.

"What a dope I am, Yeller. I'm just a smudge in the context of things. But maybe I should try to make some difference."

In bed she examined the ways she might change her lifestyle and decided there were not enough hours to do any more than she was already doing.

XIII

Friday usually was a busy day at work. Hobby and professional farmers picked up grain. The feed mill was open Saturday mornings, but Jim worked alone. On Fridays he and his other employee filled orders to be picked up that day or Saturday. It was a small, shoestring operation. If Joan could have worked there Saturday mornings, she would have.

Jim had warned her that in the afternoon the arrogant young man whose Rottweilers had bit her and Yeller was coming to pick up horse feed and that she should let him know if there was any trouble. When the dually drove up, she was busy at the counter with another customer and kept Yeller close beside her. The young man hoisted the bags and carried them to the truck. When he was done loading, he came to the counter to pay. Leaning on the scarred wood waiting for his turn, he took his ball cap off and ran fingers through dense black hair.

The other customer left and he said, "Nice dog, that one. I'm truly sorry he got bit."

Remembering his cocksure attitude, she was impatient with his apologies and said nothing.

"How are you doing?" he asked. His eyes were nearly black, surrounded by bloodshot whites.

"Better," she said.

"Do you ever work with dogs?" he asked.

"Not Rottweilers." She peered around his shoulder. "Where are they anyway?"

"Home. You wouldn't work with them then? I told my dad how well behaved your dog is."

"He's not a Rottweiler." She was mellowing a little, wondering if this was how she could make a difference.

"They ain't bad. They're just scared, and we don't have time to train them."

"What kind of horses do you have?" she asked.

"Quarter horses.

"Hmm," she said noncommittally.

He handed her a check for the feed and a business card with directions on the back. "Come see the place sometime."

* * * * *

That night she went home, put on worn slacks and an old T-shirt, apologized to Yeller for leaving him there, and drove to Liz's. The outside light was on when she arrived, and Liz met her in the yard. The puppy, a black ball of fur, ran to her and attacked her slacks with his teeth.

"It's a game of his," Liz explained, prying him from Joan's pants and carrying him inside where she put him in his kennel. As soon as the pup was shut away, the gray cat appeared and rubbed against Liz's legs. In the bright light of the kitchen Liz looked gaunt.

"Are you all right?" Joan asked.

"Fine. Are we going to Diversity?" Her eyes were such a bright blue that they looked unreal.

"David wants to meet us there. Is that okay with you?"

"Sure," Liz said. "Linda probably will be there too. Want a drink before we go? Vodka and tonic or something?"

"Make it light," she said with a half smile. "What's on your mind?"

Liz filled two glasses with ice. "There is something I want to talk about." She poured a small amount of vodka over the ice. "I want to be your friend. I like you."

Joan was puzzled. "You are my friend."

"Don't ignore me if you decide to go with Linda. I mean, we don't have to be sexual if you don't want to."

"She told you, didn't she?" she said, her face flushing. "It just sort of happened."

Liz looked sad and tired. "It just sort of happened with you and me."

140

"I initiated that."

"Tell me something," Joan said on the way to Diversity. "Do you ever feel as if your life has meant nothing?"

"Sure. I think we all do. It's that midlife crisis thing. You get to a certain age and you want to leave a mark on the world. Time's running out."

"Exactly," she murmured. "What do you do with those feelings?"

"I tell myself that when I retire I'll volunteer for everything. There's not time now. I'd go crazy keeping up with what I have to do and volunteering too." She turned her head. "And so would you."

"How old are you?"

"Forty-six, and you?"

"Fifty in September." She sighed.

"We'll have to have a party," Liz said.

"Over my dead body."

She saw David's Taurus in the parking lot and Linda's Grand Am and wanted to go elsewhere, but she'd told David she'd be here. The music and smoke hit them like a wall. They wormed their way to the bar, ordered two glasses of Merlot and two combination dinners, and went through the back door to find a couple of places at a picnic table outside.

With wineglasses in hand, they looked around the enclosed garden till David and Linda waved them over. "We saved you seats."

Linda introduced the woman next to her, whose name Joan immediately forgot but whose face she remembered from the women's potluck at Liz's house.

"Did you order?" David asked, scanning the crowd. Joan nodded and felt something brush her leg.

Looking under the table, she saw Sylvester gleaning the tidbits of fallen food. "What's he doing here?"

"I couldn't leave him at home." David said.

"Why not? I left Yeller and Liz left Buddy. I'll bet most of the people here have dogs at home."

"Not the lesbians," Linda said. "Most of them have cats."

"This is no place for a dog. It's like bringing your kid with you."

"I'd put him in the car, but somebody might steal him," David said.

"Somebody might step on him out here," Liz said.

"All right." He grabbed the dog up. "I'll hold him on my lap." But the puppy squirmed so much, he soon put him down where people fed him french fries.

"You know what happens to dogs that eat garbage?" Joan said.

"I suppose you're going to tell me they die from it," he remarked. "You're a fun person tonight, Joanie."

So she shut up. When their dinners came, he put the pup in the car with the windows down a few inches and the doors locked. It was cool enough so that he wouldn't suffer any discomfort.

"Are you staying for the dancing?" Linda asked, looking from Liz to Joan.

"I have to work tomorrow," Joan said.

"Like I said . . ." David began.

"Don't say it again," Joan snapped. "Yes, we'll stay a while."

When the beat picked up, resounding in her ears

and hitting the inner walls of her skull, Joan looked at Liz questioningly. "Want to dance?"

They made their way inside and moved in tight circles at the edge of the dance floor. Even so, couples bumped into them. "Are you having fun yet?" Joan shouted at Liz.

Liz leaned forward. "What?"

She repeated the question and Liz shook her head. "Want to go?"

"What?"

Grabbing Liz's hand she pulled her outside. They went to the table to say good-bye to David and Linda, but both were gone. In the Bronco, Joan said, "Listen. You can hear the beat out here."

On the way home, Liz said, "When I was younger, I never wanted to leave."

Joan sniffed at her clothes. "I hate smelling like a smoked cigarette." She grinned at Liz in the dark car. "Is David right? Am I no fun?"

"He was teasing."

Joan thought about how the dogs made their options difficult. She cleared her throat. "What do you want to do?"

Liz looked at her. "Whatever you want to do."

"I want to go to bed with you, but Yeller is at my place and Black Buddy is at yours."

"Let's pick up Yeller and your clothes for to-morrow," Liz said without hesitation.

Yeller's toenails skittered as he danced an awkward welcome. Joan gathered clothes for the next day along with her toothbrush, shampoo, and other necessities and stuffed them in her overnight bag, turned off lights, locked the door, and helped Yeller into the backseat.

Liz had waited in the Bronco. "It's so quiet out here," she said.

"Till Lou shows up on weekends. It'll be quieter at your place tomorrow morning. I guarantee you."

"Do you think you'll ever move again?" Liz asked.

"Because of Lou, I was thinking about it a couple of weekends ago, but unless I can afford to buy several acres, there's no way to ensure privacy or quiet. Someone could buy the lot next door and turn it into a junkyard. I've seen it happen. A real nice, well-kept property next door or across the road from a shack surrounded by abandoned cars, broken-down lawn mowers and rototillers, and some couple screaming at a bunch of kids."

Liz said, "I'm going to have to do something about my barn before the city steps in."

"Hey, maybe Lou could shore it up. He's in construction."

"I should get an estimate either way: tearing it down or fixing it," Liz said.

When they stood on either side of Liz's bed, Joan felt suddenly shy. She hadn't been in this room. It was personalized with family pictures on the wall, books and magazines piled on the floor by the bed, clothes hanging in the closet.

"I feel like your family is watching," she said.

"We can read if you want. They probably wouldn't object to that." Liz laughed. "I'm serious. I just like having you here. I get lonesome."

Joan climbed between the sheets after retrieving her book from the overnight bag. The bed was illuminated by a light attached to the headboard. "I was an only child. Maybe that's why I seldom get lonely."

Unable to concentrate, she read the same paragraph three times before moving on to the next one. When Liz touched her, she savored the caresses until Liz began removing her T-shirt and panties, at which point Joan could no longer pretend nonchalance. Liz's passion evoked her own; her demanding mouth and hands provoked desire.

"Let's go slow," she whispered as Liz reached up and turned off the light.

For background there were the crickets, one apparently in a corner of the room. The pup was in the kitchen in his kennel, but Yeller snored softly on the rug. Liz's breathing, loud in her ears, was echoed by her own. Their panting quickened, keeping pace with their bodies, rose to gasps and cries of pleasure, ended in renewed silence — except for the crickets' chirrs, the dog's snores.

They were both at the head of the bed again, Joan's arm around Liz. Joan was comfortably inside her head, thinking about what she would make for dinner at Diane's on Sunday. She wanted to talk to Diane about the arrogant young man's request, that she train his Rottweilers.

"Do you think you'll ever want to live with someone again?" Liz asked.

"My house doesn't have enough square feet to accommodate anyone else." When she bought it, she'd already decided she didn't want to live with anyone, unless it was Diane, in which case she'd have to live in Diane's house.

"Mine does," Liz murmured.

Joan absently ran fingers through Liz's curls. She

liked the soft texture, the thickness. "You've got room for the whole neighborhood."

"What are you doing after work tomorrow night?" Liz asked.

"I have to grocery shop. I'm taking dinner to Diane's Sunday night. Want to come? You can bring Black Buddy."

"Let me grocery shop with you."

"Only if you help me fix the enchiladas."

"Only if you ask me to stay over."

"Done," Joan said, coming to the conclusion that lust was at the bottom of her congeniality. Where was her need for space, for walks in the wild, for exercise? Maybe she should have bought a larger house.

Liz followed her home from the grocery store. Before going inside, Joan walked over to the lot next door and looked into the hole Lou had dug for the basement. The backhoe was parked nearby, but Lou's truck and trailer were gone.

After carrying in the groceries, she showed Liz the path she had forged to the creek. They stood on the lip of the gurgling water, swatting at deerflies and mosquitoes, and then ran back to the yard as if pursued by tigers.

"We'll have to spray next time. Even Yeller won't follow me to the creek."

Black Buddy had and was now snapping at the air and chewing on his behind. They looked at him and laughed. He was flattening the wildflowers that Joan had planted along the back of the yard.

After making the enchiladas, they ate a couple and

went outside to finish their wine. Joan was feeling a contentment she'd only experienced on rare occasions. She could get used to this companionship.

The following day at Diane and Tania's, Joan talked about the arrogant young man while they ate the remainder of the enchiladas. She and Liz had both ridden Trixie in the afternoon. Joan was tempted by the quarter horses, not the Rottweilers.

"Cortland, that's the name. He's Marland and the kid's Gene," Diane said.

"Cortland Quarter Horses." Joan dug the card out of her purse and showed it to them. "He said the Rottweilers weren't mean, they were scared."

"And a frightened dog bites," Tania finished. "You sure you want to take them on?"

"If you do, I'll go with you," Liz said. "I can help. I've taken dog obedience classes."

They all looked at her, flushed with the day's fresh air and exercise and the wine. Diane said, "I'd feel better if you did."

"So would I," Tania added.

On the way back to her house, Joan asked, "Will you go with me? I'd just like to see the place, is all. Take a look at the horses." Because of the fancy truck, she was convinced the horses would be special.

"Of course I will," Liz said. "I hate to go home tonight."

"Stay then," Joan suggested.

"I can't."

XIV

She called the number on the card from work the next day and left a message on the answering machine. At noon Gene returned the call.

"Hey, come on out tonight. Me or my dad'll show you around."

When she turned into the Cortlands' driveway, she was surprised by the modest yet efficient layout. The house was a double trailer that was dwarfed by a huge barn, an indoor riding arena, pastures, and an outdoor pen for riding. Brood mares and foals grazed in the fields divided by well-kept board fences. A six-horse side-by-side gooseneck horse trailer was parked by the barn.

Liz had been unable to come, so Joan had gone straight from the feed mill. Leaving Yeller in the Bronco with the windows open partway, she went in search of someone. The Rottweilers barked from their twin dog runs near the barn. They set up a racket that heralded her arrival, but she walked to the barn without seeing anyone.

Inside, the horses whickered to her from their stalls. They moved around, stirring up the sawdust at their feet, stretching their long necks and heads over their doors into the paved aisleway. She touched their soft muzzles and spoke to them as she walked toward the arena where someone was riding.

"Hey, it's the lady from the feed mill," Gene said from atop the gelding he was riding.

Another man brought the horse he was on to a sliding stop, then pivoted one hundred eighty degrees and rode to Joan. He had a head of thick, graying black hair, bushy eyebrows, and a lean body — Gene's older image. "You the woman them Rottweilers bit?" His voice was a low growl.

"Yep," she said. "I came out to talk to you about them."

He dismounted. "Name's Marland." He stretched a hand for her to shake. "Guess you know Gene."

"I met him not under the best circumstances." His grip was hurting her hand.

"He gets out of hand now and then. Was he a smart ass?"

"Well, sort of." She grinned, loving the way he used words and making a conscious effort not to imitate him.

"Gene, you show her them dogs. Make them mind now."

Gene dismounted and tied his mount to the rail with a rope that looped around its neck. "That's what she's here to do, Dad. They don't listen to me."

"Well, do your best. Sorry they bit you, ma'am. They shouldn't have been running loose. Gene knows better." He put a foot in the stirrup and vaulted easily into the saddle where he looked down at her for a moment. "Well, good luck. If you can't do anything with them, they'll just have to stay penned."

Gene said, "They jumped out of the truck. I never let them out." He turned to her. "Come on, ma'am. Where's your dog?"

"In the truck, waiting. It's cool enough. And call me Joan."

They walked together to where the barking dogs threw themselves at the walls of the kennels.

"Shut up," Gene shouted. He grabbed a leash hanging from one pen and opened the door to slip inside. Leashing the dog, he brought it out to where Joan waited.

"Hey, boy," she said softly. The dog lunged at her, but she held her ground, her arms at her sides, neither backing off nor moving toward him. She figured she presented a less threatening figure that way. "Let him sniff," she said in the same tone.

He snuffled around her crotch and touched her hand with his nose. Turning it over she presented it to him. In a few moments she was caressing his head. "Hey, I'm not going to hurt you. I'm one of the good guys." She looked at Gene, who was hanging on to the leash with both hands. "Let me have him."

When he handed her the leather strap, she wrapped it around her hand till the dog leaned against her. The trick was to make this animal think she was top dog. She wasn't crazy about this breed, but she'd give this a try.

"Want me to hang around?" Gene asked, looking worried.

"Yeah, this first time." She walked around with the dog at her left side, using heel commands, not jerking too hard, letting the dog get used to her voice and the choke collar and leash.

The other dog was whining to be let out. She wasn't going to be the one to do that. After a half-hour, she asked Gene to leash the other dog, and she put the first one back in his kennel.

When she had worked both dogs long enough, Gene said, "Get your dog out and I'll show you around. He won't chase them mares and foals, will he?"

"Not Yeller," she said.

They went back to the barn, and Marland joined them. He showed her their stud, told her how he was bred and about his show record. He took out the horses they were showing, the offspring of the stud and the mares in the fields, stood them up for her, and recited their achievements.

"Do you ride?" he asked.

"Yep. I showed quarter horses for a while, years ago. Can't afford to now."

He looked at her with eyes as black as his son's, but more piercing. "Want to ride a real pleasure horse?"

"I'd love to," she said.

He put her on a five-year-old gelding they had raised and shown. The horse's flatfooted easy walk, his soft trot, and his rocking horse canter were so comfortable she could have ridden all day.

"He's for sale," Marland said, spitting in the dirt of the arena. His lower lip hid a dip of snuff from the can in the back pocket of his jeans.

"How much?" she asked, knowing it would be some astronomical sum.

It was. "Thirty-five," he told her. His arms were crossed over his short-sleeve polo shirt.

"Thirty-five what?" Maybe she could dredge up thirty-five hundred. She could keep the horse at Diane's.

"Thousand." His lips curved a little. "And that's cheap for this horse."

She said "Whoa" quietly, and the horse stopped dead in front of Marland and Gene. This horse was an equine version of Yeller, but she couldn't afford a thirty-five-thousand-dollar horse. What was the point of falling in love with him?

"You ride good," Gene commented, spitting into the riding arena as his father had.

"Thanks." She dismounted and stroked the gelding's long, lovely neck. "He's a wonderful horse, but priced way out of my league." It was the jolt she needed to catapult her back into reality. Trixie was more her style, but she would have trouble supporting Trixie. Maintaining a horse took a lot of money.

When she left with Yeller, the two men were still in the barn, the windows lit against the fading light. The Rottweilers threw themselves against the walls of their kennels as she passed with Yeller at her side. Their fierce barking followed her to the Bronco.

She called Liz when she got home, asked if she wanted to go with her on Wednesday after work.

"How was it?" Liz asked.

She told her about the dogs, the horses, the two men.

"Are those dogs safe to work with?" Liz sounded worried.

"I don't know. We'll ask Gene to hang around till they're used to us. Bring Black Buddy and his kennel. You can stay over if you want."

On Wednesday, Liz met her at work and rode with her to the Cortlands', where they went looking for Gene. No one was in the barn and the trailer was gone.

"They knew we were coming," Joan said. "I'm not getting those dogs out of their kennels without Gene around." The Rottweilers stood with huge paws against the interlinking chain walls and barked.

Ten minutes later the truck and trailer pulled into the driveway and parked beside the barn. Gene got out of the truck.

"Hey," Gene called. "Sorry. I had to get the bearings packed on the trailer. Took more time than I thought." He walked toward them.

"We couldn't find your dad either."

"He left for a judges' seminar out west that starts tomorrow. He's a horse judge," he explained. "You don't have to wait for me to get them dogs out."

"Oh yes we do," Joan said, "till we know them better or they know us better." She introduced Liz. "Liz is going to help."

Gene sat on the top board of the nearest wood fence and watched till Joan told him she thought it was okay and that he could go.

"Listen, I'll be in the barn riding. Come see me before you go."

When he walked away, the dogs started to follow but were brought back to heel with a slight jerk. Joan realized the animals were smart, they learned quickly, but she would not feel successful until she commanded their complete attention. She wanted them to come when called off leash under all circumstances.

After spending an hour with the dogs, she gave them each a dog biscuit and put them in their kennels with words and pats of praise. Then she and Liz went to the barn where Gene was riding in the arena.

He was on the gelding she had ridden Monday. "Someone's coming to see him this weekend." Sliding to a stop in front of where they stood, he said, "I hate to see him go, he's such fun to ride. Why don't you take him around the arena once or twice? Give me a chance to see him go."

Joan grinned at Liz. "You'll love this horse."

Gene walked out of the barn with them after putting the gelding back in his stall. "How'd them dogs do?" he asked.

"They're quick studies," Joan said. "You shouldn't have any trouble teaching them yourself."

"I ain't no dog trainer," he said.

"Well, you could be, and it's you and your dad they're going to have to listen to."

"My dad definitely ain't no dog trainer. He thought we should shoot them after they bit you."

"You'll have to do something if you can't trust them," Liz murmured.

"That's what he'll do. I guarantee it. He ain't got no patience with dogs."

"He does with horses," Joan said.

"Horses are his livelihood. He don't want no dogs around that'll bite potential customers."

Liz said, "Makes good sense."

Gene held the Bronco door open after Joan climbed in. "Okay. You teach me, I'll become a dog trainer."

"We'll start next time, which is when, by the way?" Joan asked.

"We're busy this weekend, so how about next week Monday?" Gene slammed the door and leaned on the open window. His dark eyes gleamed with humor.

Joan drove to her house where they released Yeller and Black Buddy into the backyard. The two women sat in lawn chairs, sipping wine and swatting mosquitoes as bats flew erratically overhead. Liz ducked and grinned.

Joan asked, "Hungry yet?"

"Starved," Liz replied.

"Why didn't you say so?"

"Because this is so nice, but now I'm getting cold and hungry and mosquito bit."

They went into the brightly lit kitchen where the night was black against the open windows. But the smells drifted through the screens: grass no longer freshly cut, pines without the sun to accentuate their odor, wildflowers dampened by dew, roses under the window.

Joan opened the fridge and peered inside. She took out a block of medium cheddar, some carrots and an onion, a loaf of bread, and milk. From the cupboard she got a box of angel hair pasta. She sautéed the carrots and onion, cooked the pasta, made a white cheese sauce, and stirred it all together. They sat at the kitchen table and ate hungrily.

"I was afraid of those dogs," Liz said.

"Them dogs." Joan grinned, mimicking Gene. "Me too. I felt they could turn on us anytime. We have to teach them to never consider that an option."

"Are you sure you want to do this?" Liz asked, doubt in her eyes.

"You don't have to go with me, Liz," Joan said. "I go there as much to see the horses as anything. Wouldn't it be great to be able to do what they do for a living? Can you imagine owning a horse that might be worth thirty-five thousand dollars?"

Tormented by Black Buddy, who bit his tail whenever it moved, Yeller lay his head in her lap.

"I'll put Buddy in his kennel," Liz said. "Poor old dog."

"How's Mr. Cinders?" she asked of the Browns' puppy.

"They love him."

"Do you want to come here Saturday after work?" Joan asked.

"I thought I'd go up to the lot on the bay. Would you consider going with me again?"

"Well, it'll get me away from the construction next door. Is Linda going along?"

"If she does, you're sleeping in my tent. The dogs can have the back of the Explorer." They had eaten the last of the stir fry. "Let me help you clean up here, and then I'll go home."

"You're not going to stay?"

"Not tonight."

The phone rang and Joan let the answering

156

machine pick it up. It was Linda asking Joan if she wanted to go out for fish Friday night. Joan met Liz's eyes.

"I'm not comfortable with her," she said.

Liz shrugged and opened the kennel door. The pup tumbled onto the floor, and she picked him up as he headed for Yeller.

"Doesn't it make you angry?" Joan asked.

"Not really. If you want to be with her, you will be, no matter what I want."

"What kind of friend horns in on her best friend's . . ." She didn't know how to finish the sentence. Was she Liz's lover?

Liz picked up the kennel with her free hand. "Walk me out."

The night was still, the mosquitoes voracious. Liz quickly left and Joan hurried inside.

The house was suddenly silent, and she who thought she valued silence so much went to bed to escape it.

At work the next day she realized she hadn't returned Linda's call and decided to leave a message on her answering machine. She would go Friday night. She had no excuse not to. Liz hadn't asked her, nor had she suggested they spend that evening together.

She met Linda at Diversity where they huddled outside at a table with eight other people.

"Why did you never call me after our evening together?" Linda asked when their drinks arrived. She was scanning the crowd as David did, so she missed Joan's shrug.

"I did call and thank you," she said.

"On my answering machine. Are you afraid of me?" Linda gave her a teasing smile.

Joan considered the question and decided to be honest. "No. You puzzle me."

"Not that again." Linda looked annoyed.

"I think you want to come between me and Liz, and she's supposedly your best friend. I don't get it."

Linda laughed. "Is there something between the two of you that I could interfere with?"

"You have such nice parents," she said wistfully. "I wish you did like me, and me you, but there you go putting me off again."

"Hey, you two," David said, sitting down next to Joan. "Where's the third musketeer?"

Joan looked into his light brown eyes. "David, you sure know how to put your foot in your mouth."

Leaving Linda at Diversity, Joan went home alone and called Liz, but she got no answer. Diane phoned her and they talked about the Cortlands, their dogs, and their horses.

The next morning Joan wakened when Lou Parry unloaded the backhoe from the trailer. The sun was just up. There ought to be a law against noise so early in the day, she thought as she squeezed her eyes shut, hoping for sleep.

After a half-hour of tossing, she got up and let Yeller outside. Putting on the coffee, she waited for it to brew, then took a cup outside where she sat in a chaise longue and watched the morning take shape.

Lou waved, and she lifted her arm. He turned off

the tractor and walked over to where she sat dressed in sweats against the morning chill.

"What are you doing out here so early?" she asked.

"I'm going to start putting up the basement walls."

She looked over at the stacks of block and the gasoline-powered cement mixer. "Why do you need the tractor?"

"To haul them bags of cement out of your garage." He stood looking down at her, his hair floating around his head, his cheek still creased from sleep. "Ain't you going to offer me coffee?"

Without a word she went inside and came out with a steaming cup. "I'll be glad when you're done."

"The lot on the other side of mine sold," he said.

"I know. It'll be a regular subdivision out here." She'd sell and move, she told herself, but it was easier to think about it than do it.

XV

The bay looked different under the blue vault of sky. Instead of gray, the water was a greenish blue, the waves pinpointed by flashing bits of sunshine. Scraps of white sails dipped and sped over the sheen of water in apparent disarray, crossing the golden path laid down by the sun. Motorized boats took more direct courses.

They walked the rocky beach, looking for driftwood and exercising the dogs. Yeller swam after sticks Joan threw for him. Black Buddy barked at the old dog and bit the water slapping against the shore. When his paws got wet, he lifted them one at a time and backed away. On the north side of Liz's property was a private beach, but to the south was public land.

They had arrived around six-thirty the night before and set up camp. Instead of cooking, they'd gone to a bar with a reputation for good hamburgers and french fries. But first they'd watched the sun go down till the reds and oranges and purples reflected in the calm bay had turned smoky and disappeared into darkness.

Joan retied her hair behind her head to better hold the wisps that escaped and blew in her eyes. She squinted against the sun on water, took the stick Yeller brought her, and threw it into the depths.

He bounded toward it, sending water flying into spectrums of liquid color. Black Buddy lunged after Yeller but pulled back when the water reached his belly; he barked his longing to swim and his fear of this deceptive surface that threatened to swallow him up.

She felt the sun and warm wind on her face and bare arms and legs and, knowing she would turn red even with sunblock, welcomed the heat. It was good she didn't live in a warmer climate because she'd be out in the sun all the time, developing wrinkles and skin cancer.

Sitting on an exposed root, she shielded her eyes against the glare. Yeller bounced out of the water with the stick. She took it, threw it again, and he was off in pursuit.

Liz sat on a rock nearby. "I don't think Buddy is ever going to be a water dog. At this rate, he's going to bark his brains out before he's old enough to learn anything." Liz picked the puppy up and tried to shush him.

"Do you ever swim here?" Joan asked.

"Sure. The water's always pretty cold. Want to? I didn't bring my suit, but we could go in like this."

They waded carefully into the bay, picking their way through rocks till their feet touched sand. The water was a cold shock to Joan's sun-warmed body. When they were waist deep, Liz dove and swam. Taking a deep breath, Joan followed. Yeller swam with them, the stick still in his mouth. Buddy's barks sounded far away.

Wading in, Liz grabbed the pup and carried him to where the bottom was sandy. She lowered him in the water. His ears flattened against his head, his tail streamed behind him as he paddled toward shore. Scrambling onto the rocky beach, he shook himself and watched them from a safe distance.

On shore again, they climbed the hill and stretched out on the grass to dry. Joan fell asleep and wakened to voices. At first she thought it was Liz talking to the dogs, but then she identified Linda's voice and David's. She rolled over and sat up.

"What are you two doing here?" she asked.

"Looking for you," David said, his tone alerting her to disaster. He squatted next to her. "Tania's in the hospital. Diane asked me to find you."

She jumped to her feet so fast that dizziness engulfed her.

When Joan and David left in his Taurus, Liz was already taking down the tent and putting things in the back of the Explorer with Linda's help. Yeller was tied so that he wouldn't think of following.

"Something happened with the tractor, that's all I know," he told her as they sped south on Highway 57.

A vivid mental picture of Tania trimming the

pony's feet caused Joan to lick lips suddenly gone dry. "How? What?" Tania was too competent.

"I don't know," he said. "Diane called me and I called Linda, hoping she'd know where to find you."

An hour later they turned into Saint Elizabeth's parking lot. Joan was hurrying toward the desk to ask for Tania when she saw Diane in the corner. Something about the way she was sitting sent Joan's hopes spiraling downward.

She walked over and sat in the chair next to her. Diane was staring at something Joan couldn't see. In that moment, Joan knew the impossible had happened, that Tania was dead. Putting an arm around her friend, she drew Diane toward her. They sat slumped together for what seemed a long time, till David asked if there was something he could do.

Diane stirred and lifted her head. "They took her away. Her parents want her flown out there." Diane was so lifeless, her body slack, her voice flat, that Joan absorbed the hopelessness and found it difficult to function. "She wanted to be cremated, but nothing was in writing."

"I thought you had wills and powers of attorney," Joan said.

"We did, but we didn't preplan our funerals. Who does that?"

"Find out who took her," Joan said to David. "We'll go there."

They drove through the streets toward the funeral home. The trees were heavy with leaves, flowers bloomed in yards, people were walking their dogs or riding their bikes. David knew a gay man on the funeral home's staff. He was going to meet them there. They walked into the immaculate reception room as they were, Diane in dirty shirt, jeans, and boots, Joan in wrinkled shorts and T-shirt, David in shorts and polo shirt.

David's friend met them at the door and took them downstairs. "I'm risking my job showing her like this, so be discreet," he said. He was telling them not to draw attention to themselves in any way.

Tania, covered by a sheet, lay on her back on a steel gurney. David and the funeral director left the room, and Diane slowly pulled the sheet back, revealing by inches Tania's pale body. There were bruises that must have been inflicted before death. Her arms were smudged with grease and lay by her sides at odd angles. Her eyes and mouth were slightly open as if caught by surprise, but there was no color, no light of life behind the lids, and there was a telling slackness about the mouth. Except for the scrape on her forehead, her face was as colorless as it was expressionless.

Joan was relieved when Diane pulled the sheet over Tania. It had seemed wrong to expose her when she had no say about it. She still didn't know how this had happened and was hesitant to ask because this wasn't the Diane she knew. Diane was not this docile person, and she half expected her to blow up with rage and grief.

There was a knock on the door and the funeral director, Matt something, and David entered. Joan wanted to ask the cause of death, but she couldn't get the words out. David would know, she thought, looking at him.

It all seemed surreal to her: Tania dead on the gurney, the hushed atmosphere, the expanse of carpeting and polished furniture that gave the illusion of a home without the necessary ingredients of magazines, books, television, food.

Diane turned once to look back at Tania and allowed herself to be led out the door. Joan drove Diane's truck. David headed toward home and his dog. He would ask Liz to bring Yeller to her and, when she did, he would drive her Bronco out. Joan wouldn't leave Diane alone right now. She felt a fierce protectiveness toward her. She had thrown her overnight bag in David's car, so she had what she considered her necessaries with her: her book, toothbrush and toothpaste, shampoo.

At the clinic they were greeted by the dogs as if everything was as it had been. Wolfie stepped all over the Scottie-dachshund mix, while the little dog snarled and bit him on the legs. The other three whined and pressed against the gate, and Joan gave them all a few cursory pats before going in the door after Diane.

She saw with surprise that the day was only a little more than half over. What would they do with it? Diane hadn't said more than a few words, and those were at the hospital. The silence was oppressive.

"Do you want me to call the vet who gave you Trixie and the pony and ask him to handle the practice for a while?" she asked Diane.

Diane looked at her with bewilderment and obvious pain. "That gurney. It was so hard, so cold."

Joan's heart compressed. "I know," she whispered.

Diane sighed and turned away. "I have to do something. I can't just sit around."

And Joan assumed she was talking about her calling the vet. "There's always something to do around here," she said. The company of animals was comforting. They were always glad to see you and didn't say stupid things. "Next week you could ease back into work."

"Okay. Thanks." Diane stood, looking out the window at the barn and fields. "Think I'll go outside for a while."

Joan waited till she was gone and pressed the playback button on the answering machine. She then called Dr. Brian Stadler and told him what had happened. David had said the cause of death was a broken neck. Tania had somehow gotten caught in the power takeoff shaft while trying to clear the mower deck.

She glanced out the window and saw the gray Ford 9N parked near the fence in Trixie's pasture. It looked harmless, an old tractor and mower, but she knew many farm accidents were caused by carelessness when someone tried to free moving parts from wire or twine or vegetation.

Hanging up, she went in search of Diane and found her in the barn, standing in the dark aisle, stroking the pony's velvety nose as the dogs crowded around her legs. The dogs turned to Joan, fickle in their quest for attention.

"Diane?" she said, seeing the tears as she drew close. "Oh, Diane, I'm so sorry." Her voice dropped to a whisper as she put her arms around her oldest friend. They stood together, clinging, until Joan thought there could be no more tears left. Finally, the tears dried up, no matter the sorrow.

Yeller led Liz to them, and she stood outside their small circle, waiting to be acknowledged. But Yeller, having no knowledge of decorum, pushed himself between them.

The chores had to be done: the pony's stall cleaned and the pony turned out into the riding arena where the grass only grew under the fence, the outdoor animals fed, the cages of the two cats and one dog inside the clinic cleaned and their food and water replenished.

Diane helped with the things that needed doing, and when they were done, Liz stayed with Diane while Joan went home to get clothes for the week. She would not leave Diane's side until Diane asked her to. She called Jim Taggart from home and told him she wouldn't be at work Monday or Tuesday, that there had been a death in the family.

The next day dawned lovely, warm and sunny. Hints of fall were all around them: the sumacs turning, the days shorter, the nights a little cooler, the birds flocking for their southward migration.

Joan had lain awake most of the night in the spare bedroom, getting up on occasion to press an ear against Diane's bedroom door. She insisted that Diane take a sleeping pill, and Diane had done her bidding until Joan tried to get her to eat. Food she refused.

The next morning they sat at the kitchen table, drinking coffee, which Joan hoped would give her some energy. She was numb with exhaustion, mentally and physically.

Diane, who was staring out the window at Trixie and the pony nickering to each other over their fences, said dully, "She's just gone. I keep expecting to see her walk through the door."

She put a hand over Diane's, which lay curled on the table. "I know." There were no funeral preparations, nothing to finalize Tania's death, only the unsettling knowledge that her body was being whisked away across the country. "Do you want to go where she is? I would go with you. I could call her parents."

Diane met her eyes, and Joan forced herself not to look away from the hurt. "Would you?"

She had never talked to Tania's parents, and she cringed from a conversation with them. But finding the number, she punched it in.

The man's voice that answered was subdued. Joan identified herself as a friend of Tania and Diane and listened to the silence resonating through the telephone line. She asked where Tania's body was being taken, what funeral home.

A woman came on the line, Tania's aunt. "Don't come, don't call," she said. "We have enough grief to contend with here without you people."

Joan hung up, heavy with sadness.

Somehow she and Diane got through the week. On Tuesday Gene Cortland showed up in the morning and offered to help with the chores. He returned in the afternoon and drove the tractor out of the field and parked it behind the barn. On Wednesday Joan went to work after Diane assured her she was all right. She would start seeing four-legged patients. It would give her something to do.

David called her at the feed mill and suggested a memorial service be arranged for Tania. Many people had known her, and Diane needed to be involved in some kind of formal good-bye. His funeral director friend, Matt Morgenstein, would help Diane with the planning; he would even drive out to the clinic and talk to her there. After the conversation, Joan wondered why she hadn't thought of a service.

She struggled to shake herself free of the inertia that had seized her. If she felt this way, she could only guess at how Diane must feel. After work, she returned to the clinic and found Diane x-raying a dog that had been hit by a car. Diane looked distracted when Joan offered to help, but then allowed her to assist while she set the dog's leg.

Wednesday evening, Matt Morgenstein came out with David and Liz, and he and Diane worked out the details of a memorial service, which was planned for Saturday afternoon. Afterward, David and Liz and Linda would help cater a gathering of friends at the clinic.

Actually, most of the people who attended the service at the funeral home brought casseroles and desserts to share. The clinic and house were filled with milling people who had known Tania through her work and as a friend.

Joan stood in a corner of the kitchen with Liz. It was the first chance they'd had to talk alone since the previous weekend.

"How are you holding up?" Liz asked in a low voice.

"I was numb at first. The feeling's coming back, and it's not good."

"Imagine how it must be for Diane," Liz said.

"Awful. She keeps busy, but the nights and moments alone must be pretty bad." She glanced across the room and saw David talking to Linda, and Diane in conversation with Brian Stadler, the other veterinarian, and knew this memorial service and gathering had been the right thing to do. "I keep wishing time away. I know it gets better."

"It does." Liz searched her face. "Look. Can I help somehow? Check up on your house, come out and see you?"

"That'd be nice. I felt isolated this past week. I wonder if Diane did?"

"Last weekend before all this happened," Liz said, studying her face as if looking for reassurance, "I was having a really good time."

"Me too. This still doesn't seem real." It was similar to when her parents had died, she thought. Maybe it was sudden, unexpected death that was so hard to grasp.

When she went to her solitary bed that night, Joan thought of how her life had changed in a split second. Where did Liz fit into it now, or Linda? Her focal point was Diane, until Diane no longer needed her. She steered her thoughts safely away from all the years she had silently loved Diane.

Winter

XVI

The last of the leaves fell in a torrent of wind and rain November 2, ending an unusually long, warm fall. The first snow drifted down at the beginning of December, covering everything with a heavy six-inch white blanket that brightened the barren landscape. The holidays arrived, unwelcomed, anticipated with dread, and somehow everyone got through them. January was now half over and, for Joan, time had slowed to a crawl.

When work ended and she went to her car, only the dusk-to-dawn light in the parking lot held back the icy night. She drove to the clinic, where Diane had hired a young veterinarian looking for a place to do his residency.

The first few weeks after Tania's death Joan had considered taking courses to qualify her as a veterinary assistant. She had never mentioned these thoughts to anyone, had never moved to put them into effect. They became moot when Eric Bennet arrived in late October, although Diane was not always pleased with him.

Joan had yet to move back home. Somehow the days had strung together, stretching into months. Diane had said a number of times how nice it was to have Joan there, how lonely it would be without her, so Joan had stayed on. They had fallen into a comfortable pattern: doing chores together after Joan returned from work and the clinic closed, fixing dinner afterward, reading or watching TV, and retiring to their separate bedrooms to sleep.

On Sundays Joan went to her own house, where she did whatever needed doing. It no longer felt like home to her. Next door Lou Parry's completed two-story house rose starkly out of the bare ground. A For Sale sign announced its availability. Construction had begun on a residence in the lot on the other side of the white house. Lou was in the process of restoring Liz's barn.

Joan was working only two Saturdays a month at Birds of a Feather. The other two Saturdays and Wednesday evenings she and Liz exercised horses for Marland Cortland, where the Rottweilers were obedient testimony to the women's training skills. Marland Cortland had said, "Forget the dogs. Why not help with the horses?"

She was beginning to think her personal life had come to an impasse. Diane moved through the days on automatic, and Joan felt it would be dishonest and unfair to take advantage of her friendship. Besides, she became mentally paralyzed whenever she considered a romantic move in that direction.

Liz had been patient for months now, and Joan wondered how much longer that would last. She knew Liz spent a lot of time with Linda when they weren't at the Cortlands' working horses together.

Parking at the clinic, Joan let herself into the house. Yeller padded on her heels. The lights in the barn and the absence of the dogs told Joan that Diane was out there. Grabbing her coverall off the wall by the back door and stepping into it, she and Yeller walked toward the barn.

When she neared the building, she heard voices. She had wondered about the strange pickup in the parking lot. As she went into the barn, the dogs met her. Yeller growled deep in his throat as they greeted her, each pushing in front of the other. Trixie stood in the crossties, her breath a halo around her head.

Diane introduced the two strangers as mother and daughter, saying they were interested in buying Trixie.

Stung, Joan hid her feeling of betrayal until they left promising to be back Sunday to ride the mare.

"I want you to ride her first, Joanie," Diane told her as she put Trixie in a stall.

"You never said you were thinking of selling her," she said.

"I know. I never thought of it till they brought their dog to the clinic and asked where they might find a gentle, broke horse." Diane gave her a ghost of a smile. "I would have talked it over with you."

Joan said, "But why?"

Diane leaned against the wood stall, her hands in the pockets of her coverall. "We never ride her. The girl wants a 4-H horse. Trixie would be perfect."

"He'd miss her," she said, nodding at the pony. She was angry and didn't know why.

"Well, she wasn't going to take her away. She wanted to board Trixie here. You could help her ride."

"Oh," she said, deflated, then admitted, "She would make a good 4-H horse."

Diane smiled and squeezed her arm. "Come on, let's get out of this cold."

"You've done everything already?"

"Yep. I don't know about you, but I'm hungry and tired."

Inside, they moved around the warm kitchen together. Joan fixed a salad while Diane peeled potatoes and heated up leftover meatloaf in the microwave oven.

"I'm almost afraid to tell you Brian Stadler wants two of the dogs."

Joan asked. "Which ones?"

"The Labs. He thinks they'll make good hunting dogs. I told him it might be too late in their lives, but he believes they'll be naturals. They do love water." Diane gave her an imploring look. "I'm always on the lookout for good homes for the animals. You never know when more will be dropped on the doorstep."

When they sat down, Joan asked, "What *are* your plans, Diane?"

Diane looked at her plate, chewed on her upper lip, and shrugged. There was such a dispiritedness about her that it tore at Joan's insides.

"Be honest with me," Joan said, although she

realized the truth might be something she didn't want
to hear.

Diane looked away. "I don't know if I can stay on
here, Joanie. Everything brings back memories. I
might sell the practice and either join another or start
a new one somewhere else."

Joan reached for her hand. "Couldn't you hang on
at least a year? It will get better. I promise."

"But your life is on hold too, Joanie. You need to
get on with it." Diane made a sandwich out of their
hands.

"Don't worry about me. I'm doing what I want to
do."

"All right. One year," Diane promised.

Joan left Yeller home when she and Liz went to
the Cortlands. The Rottweilers met them when they
arrived and escorted them to the barn. The dogs were
happier, more trusting. A well-trained dog was like a
child with a structured life, Joan thought. Both
welcomed boundaries they recognized.

The horses they exercised were five-year-old mares
that neither Marland nor Gene had time to ride
between shows. When these mares had accumulated
enough senior western pleasure points, they would be
bred. They were so well-broke the riding was a mere
formality to keep them in shape.

"Why don't you come over to my place after work
Saturday?" Liz asked. They were trotting down the
long wall of the chilly arena toward the gate.

The times Liz had asked her over since Tania's
death, Joan had suggested that she come to Diane's

instead. After dinner, Liz had gone home alone or with Linda, who had also been invited.

"I miss you," Liz added, then put the mare into a canter, her strides lengthening the distance between them.

Liz was never pushy, never demanding. It was what Joan liked best about her. She would go. At least, she would mention it to Diane and judge from her reaction.

When Joan did tell Diane, they were in the barn feeding and cleaning stalls. Diane was raking sawdust back in place after forking out the manure. Shutting the door behind the pony, she went to get hay.

Joan carried buckets to the water hydrant and filled them. "If you don't want me to go, I won't."

"Go, Joanie. I like Liz." Diane threw the hay over the stall doors and went for grain for the mare. She would give a handful to the pony.

Joan passed her, her neck stretched under the weight of five gallons of water in each hand. "I love you," she muttered as she passed.

When they went inside, they took turns showering. They were meeting David and Guy at Diversity for fish.

On the drive there, Diane said, "I love you too, Joanie. You know that. You're my best friend."

"But you don't think of me any other way, do you?" Joan asked, her hands sweaty on the wheel. She had waited so long, but now, for some reason, she had to know.

"There's this hole inside me, like I've lost a vital part. I can't think about anybody any other way right now, especially you." Diane turned toward her. "Part of it is guilt, because I loved you too much when I was with Tania. I was even jealous of Liz."

Joan froze in place, except for her heartbeat that jumped into fast forward. This was what she had waited to hear, yet she knew Diane wasn't telling her that she wanted her. Quite the opposite, she was saying that it was now impossible for them to be together. They turned into Diversity's parking lot. This was the first time Diane had been here since Tania's death.

Diane said, "I think we both need a fresh start. Give Liz a chance. You have a lot in common."

"What if it's you I want?" she asked, parking and turning off the engine.

"It won't work. You'd be a constant reminder."

"But I knew you before you knew Tania." Joan no longer cared if what she said hurt.

"It doesn't matter." Diane reached across the seat and took her hand. "Let it go. We'll always be good friends, best friends. Perhaps that's more lasting than the other."

Joan jerked her hand away, got out of the Bronco and breathed in the cold air. She crossed her arms and blinked at the dark skies. Far above the lights of the parking lot, clouds hung in shredded fragments.

"Come on," Diane said. "We'll go play let's pretend. It's what I do every day."

It knocked the meanness out of Joan. In the smoky interior, who would notice if her eyes watered or were red? She took Diane's arm.

Inside, they found David and Guy already at a

table in the bar. The two men got to their feet and pulled out chairs. "Where have you been?" David asked. "I was getting worried."

"Chores," Diane said, sitting down with a smile as if all was right with her world.

I can do that too, Joan thought. "You only have one dog to feed," she pointed out.

Guy went to get drinks, and David leaned forward to whisper loudly, "We're friends, nothing more. So don't ask."

"Fuck it all," Joan said in mutual sympathy.

He gave an exaggerated shrug. "My feelings exactly."

When Liz and Linda came in, David moved over to make room for them.

"Join us," he said.

Joan met Liz's eyes and nodded. Her smile twisted on her face, and she got up to go to the restroom.

Liz found her locked in a stall and waited, leaning against a sink. "What is it?"

Joan came out and washed her hands in the next sink. "I'll be at your house tomorrow after work."

"What happened?" Liz asked.

"Not a goddamn thing."

"You look like you've been crying. If you don't want to come, don't." Liz was looking at her in the mirror.

"It's the smoke." She splashed water on her face.

"Yeah, sure." Liz put a hand on Joan's shoulder and left.

She'd tell her tomorrow, maybe, but who wants to know they're second choice?

On the way home she said little and, when Diane again reached for her hand, she squeezed back, thinking there was some peace in letting go, in having no expectations.

It was black, cold, and quiet until they reached the clinic. Brian Stadler had taken the two Labs that day, and the greeting they received was more subdued. The dogs stayed in the mud room when the nights were cold, except for Yeller who waited inside.

In bed, Joan considered going to Diane's room for one last try, but Tania was as much there as she had been when she was alive. Diane would have to come to her room, and she realized how telling it was that she never had.

Joan lay with hands under her head and watched the shadows of tree branches bend on her ceiling and walls. Here she didn't rail against the dusk-to-dawn lights, and there were two: one out by the barn and one in the parking lot.

The next morning she packed a bag before she left for Birds of a Feather. "What are you going to do today?"

"What I do every day," Diane answered. She looked tired. "Will you be back Sunday afternoon to ride Trixie for those people?"

"Sure." She slung her bag from her shoulder. "Call if you need me."

"Say hello to Liz." Diane kissed her on the cheek, eliciting quick tears.

It was like saying a final good-bye for some reason, and she got out of the house in a hurry. At the store, she turned up the heat, switched on the CD player, counted the change, and opened the door.

The place was often a zoo on winter Saturdays. Cabin fever created shoppers trying to banish winter blues, and people bought seed and feeders and

181

browsed. At noon Kathy dropped in and stayed because there were so many customers.

"You look terrible," Kathy remarked when there was a lull in traffic.

"Thanks," Joan said dryly.

"Maybe you need more time off," Kathy suggested.

"Maybe I need to be busier," she countered.

"What's going on?" Kathy asked. "Is Diane all right?"

"No. I don't know. She goes through the motions."

"Tania's been dead how long? Five months. That's not long in the scheme of things." Kathy's hair, full of static electricity, flew out from her head.

"I know. It just seems like a long time." Perhaps a year from now Diane would feel differently about her. Joan was suddenly ashamed of her own selfishness. Instead of mourning Tania's death, she was unhappy because Diane was unable to consider her romantically. She shook herself.

"I'm sorry," she said. "I can be such an asshole."

"Can't we all," Kathy replied.

She and Yeller left the store at five-forty-five and drove through dark streets to Liz's house. The barn was under construction and stood starkly naked of much of its siding, propped up by new two-by-fours. Getting out of the Bronco, she and Yeller stood for a moment, breathing in the frigid air and silence.

Yeller leaned companionably against her leg, and she realized he had suffered neglect too in the months that followed the accident. "I'll be more attentive," she promised, briefly craving the quiet. Now it seemed a short time since Tania's death and the wait for Diane to stop grieving just beginning.

The outside porch light came on, casting a yellow

circular glow over Liz on the steps and the snowy yard beyond. Black Buddy raced toward the Bronco, then faltered to an uncertain stop. She realized he didn't recognize them in the dark and called him by name, whereupon he turned into a wriggling ball of welcome.

She laughed. It was good to be here where there were no ghosts, no lingering aura of death.

XVII

Liz grinned, holding the door open as Joan and Yeller went inside. Buddy squeezed past them, and Yeller growled at his bad manners. The warm kitchen smelled of bread baking and food in the oven, and Joan's stomach clenched in hunger. She caught sight of the gray cat vanishing into the pantry.

"Is that where she goes?"

"That's where her food and water are. I have to hide the food behind a wall of cans or Buddy eats it."

"How do they get along?"

"Okay. She bats him on the nose if he gets too familiar." Liz cocked her head. "How are you tonight?"

"Hungry, ready to sit down. What is it that smells so good?"

"Beef burgundy." An open bottle of Merlot stood on the kitchen table, which was set for two. Liz poured two glasses and sat down with Joan. "Lou is almost ready to put the siding back on the barn. He'll be out there tomorrow morning."

"I can't get away from him, can I?" she said. The wine tasted wonderful, quickly relaxing her. She leaned back in the chair and sighed deeply in pleasure. Yeller laid his head on her knee and ignored the puppy chewing on his legs.

Liz picked up the little dog and put him in his kennel where he let out a grievous yowl. "I wanted to bounce some thoughts off you."

"What?" Joan asked, scratching behind Yeller's ears.

"When Lou finishes, I think I'm going to put the place on the market." Liz held up a hand when Joan frowned. "The upkeep is horrendous, and I long for a warm, sunny house with an open concept. But I wanted to talk with you first."

"Why?" Joan asked, perplexed.

"I want to live with you."

Joan's hand paused in mid stroke. "Oh," she said and then the phone rang.

Liz snatched it off the wall. "What?" She sounded annoyed. "I have company right now." A short pause. "Yes. I'll talk to you tomorrow." And she hung up.

"That was Linda. She's going out with Lou, believe it or not."

185

Joan was quiet for a moment, unable to absorb this. "You're serious, aren't you?"

"Yep. She thinks he's cute."

"He is in an ugly sort of way," Joan agreed. "She really is bisexual then."

"So she says." Liz rested her chin in her hand. "Can we forget her for now?"

She almost told Liz then how she felt about Diane, how she wanted to give her time, how she didn't feel as if she could leave her right now, but in the end she said nothing. It all seemed pointless.

When they moved into the living room after dinner, the conversation was still sidetracked. While Liz fed more wood to the flames in the fireplace, Joan looked around at the dark corners. No wonder Liz wanted something light and airy. For a moment Joan missed her own home, wanted to return to its cozy warmth.

Instead of sitting next to her, Liz took a nearby chair and leaned forward, arms on legs, hands dangling.

Uh-oh, Joan thought.

"What do you think about us living together? Will it ever happen?" Liz's eyes looked dark in the dim light.

Leaning back and crossing her arms, Joan stared into the fire. "I don't know. I never thought about it."

"I mean, we could be roommates, but we'd have to find a house that suited us." Liz sat up straight. "Who am I fooling? You're not looking for another house; you're living with Diane. Sorry."

"Maybe the three of us should live together," Joan said in an attempt to lighten things up.

Liz looked at her and snorted. "Or the four of us.

We could ask Linda." She leaned forward again, and Joan stiffened. "Is there something between you and Diane?"

She didn't know how to answer. "Yes, no. I've always loved Diane, just as you love Linda."

"As a friend?" Liz persisted.

"She says she can't be any more," Joan said dully, keeping her gaze on the fire.

"But you want more?" Liz wouldn't let it go.

"I thought if I gave her enough time she would maybe be able to see me that way."

"I see." Liz leaned back again and heaved a sigh. "Do I just wait then and see if she comes around? In the meantime, do we make love?"

Joan glanced at her and away as desire flooded her. "It's up to you."

"I'll be right back." Liz left the room.

When Liz returned, she was carrying a portable mattress, a few inches thick, and a couple of quilts, all of which she dropped on the floor in front of the fire. She covered the mattress with one quilt, took the pillows off the couch and threw them on top. Turning off the lights, she stretched out a hand and said, "Come on."

Slowly, Joan got up, covered the few feet between them and stood obediently while Liz pulled off her sweater and unzipped her jeans. When Joan tried to finish undressing herself, Liz took her hands and put them at her sides.

"Let me," Liz said, kneeling to pull her pants and underwear down.

When she was naked, Joan lifted Liz's sweater over her head and watched her hair fan out in an electrostatic halo. Reaching behind Liz, she unhooked her bra and held the weight of her breasts in her hands, letting Liz worm out of her own jeans. All the while, her mind tried to put Diane in Liz's place.

Liz covered them with the other quilt, and the heat of the fire baked Joan's face, even as her backside cooled. Shadows leapt across the walls and ceilings as the fire crackled and pulsed blue and red and yellow.

"I love you," Liz murmured.

Joan replied, "I want you." That was honest enough.

Afterward, Liz fed the flames again, and they lay quietly basking in the heat till Joan fell asleep. She awoke in the night, disoriented and having to pee. The fire was embers, the room cold and black.

"Let's go to bed," Liz said, her voice throaty with sleep.

Joan gathered her clothes and followed Liz up the stairs.

Wakening in the morning to hammering, Joan opened her eyes to sunshine. She got up on one elbow and looked at Yeller, who was looking at her. The puppy would be bursting. Loathe to leave the warm nest of bed, she gazed around for something to put on.

Downstairs, she took the pup out of his kennel and put both dogs outside while she watched from the storm door. Lou Parry was on a ladder, nailing a barn board to the new two-by-fours. He wore a knitted cap, a hooded sweatshirt, a coverall suit, gloves, and boots. Reluctantly, she made coffee to take to him when all she wanted to do was return to bed. Carrying a cup outside, she saw him drinking from his thermos.

"Brought my own," he said, "but yours is fresher."

She couldn't picture him with Linda. He was too short, too homely, too unintellectual.

"What are you doing here anyway?" he asked. A strand of blond hair escaped the cap and fluttered in the cold breeze.

Shrugging an answer, she said, "Any bites on selling your house?"

"I'm gonna move in," he said. "Take that For Sale sign down, will you?"

"Sure." She edged toward the house, calling the dogs. "I'm going inside now."

Upstairs, she climbed back in bed with Liz, who put warm arms around her.

She invited Liz to go with her to ride Trixie for the mother and daughter. After a little coaxing, Liz agreed. They drove two cars, so that Liz could return home on her own. The strange pickup was in the parking lot, and Joan hurried out to the barn while Liz put Buddy in his kennel in the house.

The barn offered cold shelter from the wind. Trixie stood crosstied in the aisle while the girl and her mother brushed her, and Joan paused in the doorway to draw breath. She felt a pang of remorse for having willingly deserted Trixie for the Cortlands' horses.

"There you are," Diane said, coming out of Trixie's stall with the wheelbarrow and pitchfork. She introduced the mother and daughter as Elaine and Susie.

At the end of the barn was a small exercise pen, hardly big enough to call a riding arena, barely large enough to walk, trot, and canter. The dust rose under Trixie's hooves in tiny puffs, separating the surface from the frozen ground. Trixie tossed her head and sidestepped when Joan threw a leg over the saddle. Joan spoke to her quietly, steadied her with the reins,

189

made contact with her legs — "Easy, girl, calm down and show these people your stuff" — until she felt the mare relaxing under her.

When it came time for Susie to ride, Joan stood by, holding the reins while the girl mounted. "Take her over to the rail and ride. I'll stand in the middle here and coach."

At first the girl looked like a sack on the horse's back, her heels creeping up with each jounce. As she followed Joan's shouted suggestions — "Sit up straight," "Get your heels down," "Keep your legs under you," "Hold your hands still" — the girl almost appeared to be in command until Trixie skidded to a stop, sending Susie forward to land on the horse's neck. If Joan hadn't been amazed at the sliding halt, she would have laughed.

"How'd you manage that?"

The girl slid off the side of Trixie's neck and landed on her feet. Her mother came running, as did Diane, and Susie said, "I love her, Mom."

"Do you want to ride, Elaine?" Diane asked.

The woman looked fearful and mounted Trixie as if the horse were a bomb about to explode. Joan stood in the middle of the arena, lifting one frozen foot and then the other as she gave instructions. She felt sorry for the woman, who bounced around and clung to the saddle, and for Trixie, who was clearly bewildered by conflicting cues.

When Joan put the mare back in her stall, she heard Diane tell the mother and daughter to take their time in making a decision, that the horse wasn't advertised and she wouldn't sell her out from under them. "Talk it over. She'll still be here."

Liz had brought leftover beef burgundy, and Diane heated it up in the microwave oven while potatoes boiled on the stove and Joan ripped up lettuce for a salad.

"They don't know the first thing about horses," Joan said. She hated turning Trixie over to such amateurs.

"You can teach them." Diane put dishes on the table. "No one's born an expert."

"Why would they want a horse when they obviously know nothing about riding?" Joan asked.

"Because little girls love horses," Liz suggested.

"Tell her about Linda, Liz," Joan urged.

"She's dating Lou Parry, who's rebuilding my barn," Liz told Diane.

"Who's he?" Diane asked, as if more surprised by the change of topic than that Linda was dating a man.

"He's the guy who bought the lot next to mine and cut down most of the vegetation before building a huge house," Joan reminded her.

"He's renovating my barn now," Liz said. "Actually, I kind of like him."

Joan looked at Liz and felt desire again. It confused her. "He's just ignorant."

"Everyone whose thinking isn't environmentally correct you consider uninformed," Diane said. "Some just don't care."

"He better. He's moving in."

Monday after work, Joan went back to Diane's to find Diane and Eric still at work. She cleaned stalls, fed and watered the animals, and returned to the house as Diane finished up in the clinic and Eric drove away.

"I'm selfish to want to keep you here, Joanie," Diane said as she sat down tiredly to take her boots off. "I think you should go home. Eric can help in the barn if I need someone."

"You have to pay him," she protested. Part of her wanted to leave behind the frustration even as she argued to stay.

Diane shrugged. "I should be paying you. You haven't slept in your own house since summer." Since Tania died.

"I'll sell it." But she didn't want to sell it.

Diane said gently, "No. You go home. I'll be fine, I promise. If I'm not, I'll let you know."

She turned up the heat and wandered through the rooms of her house, trying to make it her own again. They lived lonely lives: Liz, Diane, Linda, herself, David, Lou. It was stupid, this need to be independent. Angry with Diane for not needing her, she considered moving in with Liz. But that would be making a commitment; Liz would not be just a roommate. She knew better.

She called Liz and reminded her that the next day they would meet at the Cortlands' after work.

"I can't make it. I called Marland and talked to Gene," Liz said.

"Why didn't you tell me?" She had no wish to ride alone in the cold night.

"I'm going to be gone for a while. Where are you anyway? I left a message on Diane's machine."

Joan felt disoriented, as she did when she wakened in the night at someone else's house. "I moved back home."

"Linda and I are going to Mexico for a week's vacation. She had it planned with another friend and now that person's sick, so I'm going in her place."

Joan said the first thing that came to mind, "Where in Mexico?"

"Puerto Vallarta. Ever been there?"

"No. I've been to Ixtapa and Cancún. Who's going to take care of Black Buddy?"

"Lou is." Liz sounded far away, as if she were already gone.

"When did all this happen?" she asked. It was only Tuesday, two days from when she'd last seen Liz.

"Sunday night and Monday."

There was a space of silence during which Joan wanted to ask to go with them. She suddenly longed for warmth and sun, and she resented being shucked off like a husk of corn. "I would have watched him for you," she said stiffly.

"Lou offered."

"Well, have a good time."

"Joan," Liz said urgently, "I wish I were going with you."

Joan sighed. "I wish I were going too."

"Next time maybe."

On Wednesday she drove to the Cortlands' alone and rode both mares. Gene was riding a three-year-old gelding but left to eat while she was saddling up the second mare. Her breath enveloped her head in a warm vapor that quickly cooled. Soft whickers as one horse called to another, the mare's grunts, her breathing, her muffled hoofbeats, and the creaking of the leather saddle were the sounds of the night.

As she was passing toward her car, Gene stepped outside and asked her in for a cup of hot chocolate. She went partly out of curiosity and partly because she was in no hurry to go home. The double trailer was cozier than she would have thought possible. In one corner of the living room a fire burned in a Ben Franklin–type stove. Shelves held scores of quarter horse trophies, and every wall boasted photographs of Marland and Gene with horses. There was no woman in sight.

She sat on a leather couch and sipped the hot chocolate Gene brought her, while Marland talked about horses and shows and judging. They had just returned from a Florida circuit and would be off on the weekend for another four-day show somewhere south. This was their life. The Rottweilers, who would go along to guard the tack and feed, lay panting at her feet. A hired hand took care of the horses left behind.

"Well, I better go," she said when her cup was emptied. "Thanks."

"Wait. I owe you money," Marland said. "It won't take a minute." He went into a room down the hall and came back with a fistful of bills.

She stared at the wad he handed her. "Why don't you write a check?"

He shrugged wide shoulders. "Too much bother. It ain't enough to count. Besides, you have to share it with your friend."

She fingered the bills. He paid her and Liz fifteen dollars an hour. "Riding those mares is a pleasure." Tonight, though, it had been a lonely task.

"Beats paying for the privilege of owning one, don't it?"

She nodded. Sometimes she thought he talked like he did to sound like the cowboy he wanted to be. "Thanks. See you."

Gene said, "I'll walk you to your car."

The snow crunched and squeaked underfoot. It was so cold it hurt to breathe. "Bet you'll be glad to go where it's warm?" she said longingly.

"Yep." He hunched into a sheepskin-lined denim jacket and thrust his hands deep into his jeans. "Look. My dad never let no one ride the horses except me till you and Liz came along."

It was a compliment, she realized. "Really?"

"You got good hands and legs, both of you." He was talking about riding, not their figures.

She grinned. "And to think I thought you were an arrogant son of a bitch. Shows you how wrong a first impression can be."

He spat onto the frozen ground. She was surprised how white his teeth were despite the snuff. "I was. You took me down a peg."

She touched his arm with her gloved hand before climbing into the Bronco. "You're okay."

Shutting the car door behind her, he raised a hand, "See ya."

XVIII

Joan dusted off her cross-country skis and boots. She called Diane and asked if Yeller could spend the weekend with her, said she was going skiing at Winter Park outside Minocqua.

Before the conversation ended, she relented and asked, "Do you want to come? Eric could take care of things there."

"Yes," Diane said. "I'll ask him."

Joan's anger, her feelings of abandonment, dissolved in astonishment. She had counted on skiing to burn it away. Off the phone, she said to Yeller,

"Sorry, old boy. I hope you don't think you're abandoned." Dogs were not allowed on the trails or in most motels.

They left before dawn in Diane's van. Joan carried with her the sight of Yeller's sad eyes watching her leave. Eric would stay the night in Diane's house, taking care of the animals.

Diane glanced at Joan across the cold, dark vehicle. The sky was just beginning to lighten, a gray and rose flush across snowy fields. "He'll be just fine. Eric loves dogs, and Yeller's a prince among dogs. He won't want to part with him." Her breath hung between them.

Joan nodded and looked out the side window, trying to dispel Yeller's image. Snow was predicted for that night, but by then they would have put in a full day of skiing. "Liz went to Mexico with Linda."

"She never said anything about it last Sunday."

"She's going in someone else's place. I wish I were."

"Why aren't you?" Diane asked.

"She said she wanted to live with me, and then she goes to Mexico with Linda." Almost imperceptably dawn lifted the shade on a landscape of snow so white it dazzled eyes, so heavy it bowed limbs.

Diane threw her a look. "Let's back up to where she said she wanted to live with you. How did that come about?"

Joan shrugged. "Do you think she meant it?"

"I don't know. What was the context?"

"She talked about selling her house and us buying one together."

"Do you love her?" Diane asked.

"Do you care?" Unfair, uncalled for, but there it was at the tip of her tongue.

"Of course I care. I hope you know that," Diane snapped.

Joan turned her head toward her best friend. "I love you."

"You think you do. Not to change the subject, but did you make reservations?"

Joan laughed. "I did."

They checked into a motel on Highway 51 and Lake Minocqua before heading toward Winter Park. At ten A.M. they bought trail passes and snapped their boots in their bindings. Diane strode ahead across the field toward the line of trees where the trail heads began. She had skied the Birkebeiner race twice to Joan's once.

If there was snow anywhere in the Midwest, it would be here or in the Upper Peninsula. The well-groomed trails were wide enough to accommodate skate skiers. Although the hills were often steep and the trails ran through miles of woods, there were never trees in the middle of a trail on a downhill run as there were so often at other places.

The quiet of the forest closed around them. Even though there were many skiers on the trails, Joan felt as if they were alone. The snow and trees muffled sound. As she attempted to keep up with Diane, she heard her own rasping breath, the swish of her skis on the snow, a nuthatch muttering as it went down a tree.

Occasionally Diane stopped long enough for Joan to catch up. At noon they sat on a log by the side of the trail and ate the sandwiches Joan had packed that morning and the trail mix Diane had brought.

A man in a blue jumpsuit skate-skied toward them, his poles and skis flashing in the white on black of snow and woods. He called hello as he sped past.

"I'd like to try that," Diane said.

"I'd never be able to keep up with you then," Joan said. "You ski like there's a demon after you."

"There is." Diane's cheeks and nose were red; wisps of dark hair escaped her knit cap.

She steeled herself against empathy. "If you don't slow down, you'll kill me and I'll haunt you."

Diane laughed, the sound echoing off the trees in the white woods. She drank from the plastic water bottle they shared and handed it to Joan. "Ready to hit the trail?"

"I guess."

They skied to the warming house around four o'clock as the light fled the sky and shadows crawled over the snow. Joan's arms and groin and legs ached. She was falling from fatigue and saw that Diane was stumbling too. It was time to quit. Inside the primitive building, cast-off clothing steamed. They walked stiffly to the john and then stood in line waiting for hot cocoa.

Once Joan sat down, she thought she'd be unable to get up. The chocolate warmed her insides as well as her hands, which were curled around the cup. Diane's hair stuck up comically when she pulled her knit cap off. Joan's head itched, and she scratched it vigorously.

"I suppose I look as bad as you do?" Diane said with a wry smile.

She grinned back. "I think you look worse."

"Where do you want to eat?" Diane asked.

"Maybe we should go lie down first," Joan said, although she suspected she might not get up if she did.

Their room was on the second floor overlooking the parking lot. Night had fallen by the time they climbed the outer staircase to the long, narrow porch fronting the building and unlocked the door. Heat rushed out to greet them, and they closed the door behind them and turned on lights. Sitting down on one of the double beds, Joan groaned as she untied her ski boots with clumsy fingers. Then stripping to her long underwear, she lay spread-eagled on the brown-patterned bedspread.

"I think I've died and gone to heaven," she said without thinking.

But Diane, who lay motionless on the other bed, only said, "Me too."

When Joan awakened, she looked over at Diane and saw that she still slept. It was seven-thirty. If they were to get dinner, they'd have to hurry. She suspected most restaurants stopped serving around eight-thirty. Her stomach had collapsed in her midriff.

She got up and gingerly moved her sore muscles. They hurt to the touch. Going to the bathroom, she peed, washed her hands and face, and brushed her hair, which flew dryly away from her scalp. She tied it back in a loose ponytail. When she came out, Diane was sitting up.

They ate across the street at Bosaki's, which was crammed with snowmobilers. They asked for a table by the windows overlooking the lake and then waited in the bar half an hour before being seated. It was so dark out they couldn't see past the light on the dock below.

Joan had a thirst that couldn't be quenched. She drank glass after glass of water before sipping her wine. "I feel like somebody's been beating me," she said.

"I'll give you a rub when we get back," Diane promised.

Galvanized by the casual offer, Joan hardly tasted the broccoli soup, the strip steak, and fries. She ignored the overwhelming tiredness that threatened to consume her.

They walked back to their room, sprinting across the road along with two snowmobiles, which roared past them and disappeared down the side road next to the motel. Before climbing the steps, Joan threw her head back to look at stars glittering across the vast expanse of sky.

In undershirt and panties, Joan lay on her belly while Diane's strong hands worked her over. She winced at the firm touch, her muscles cringing.

"You act like this is torture," Diane said, sitting cross-legged at her side.

"Let me massage you," Joan said, rolling over.

"I won't argue." Diane plopped facedown on the bed.

"I should be in better shape than this," Joan mused, pressing Diane's back with the heels of her hands. "I mean, I ride twice a week."

"Different muscles," Diane muttered into the pillow. "God, that feels good."

Joan worked up Diane's back, across her shoulders, and down her arms, and found herself focusing on the nape of her neck. It was so white, so defenseless. She bent to kiss it. Diane went very still. Running strong fingers upward through Diane's hair, Joan saw Diane's flesh ripple in response.

Slowly, Joan turned her over and looked for permission. Diane's face was expressionless, her eyes dark and unreadable, but at the base of her throat her pulse beat wildly. Joan's eyes were drawn to the movement of blood through artery. She touched it with a finger, bent to brush it with her lips, and then moved up Diane's neck to her chin, to her mouth, where she tasted her lips between her own, wet them with a flicker of tongue.

Carefully, Joan lowered her body onto Diane's, displacing her weight to her elbows. The kissing took her breath away, and she had to tell herself to inhale, so intense were her efforts, so afraid she might offend. As yet, Diane had not responded.

Sliding a little to one side, she ran a hand over Diane's small breasts, her concave belly, and was enthralled to find her panties soaked with desire. Flattening her hand, Joan slipped it under the elastic and followed the liquidy path inside. Diane's moan trailed in the wake of her fingers.

Joan tasted tears in the corner of her mouth. At first she thought it was the mixing of saliva from their tongues. But then she raised her head and saw Diane's face shimmering wetly. Heart plummeting, she rolled away.

"Sleep with me tonight," Diane whispered, curling up against her back.

* * * * *

202

Moving gingerly the next morning, she went down to the motel office to get coffee and brought it to the room. Diane sat up and looked at her out of puffy eyes. Reaching for the black cup, she took a sip.

"Are you up to another day of skiing?" she asked Joan.

"If you are, I am," Joan replied, propping up pillows and leaning back against them to drink her coffee. "Look," she said. "I'm sorry about last night."

"Don't be. It confirmed something for me," Diane said.

"What? That we can't be lovers?" she asked.

"Yes. I have to let that possibility go, and so do you."

"I thought you already had." Joan's heart ached as much as her body did. She felt heavy with fatique.

They drove to the American Legion State Forest and skied the trails. Here there were sharp curves to be negotiated during downhill runs, and Joan found herself falling because her muscles were responding sluggishly. They skied past frozen lakes seen through black trees. The snow that hadn't materialized the night before began falling, dense white flakes accumulating under their skis, cutting short their plans.

Yeller frolicked clumsily in Diane's kitchen, not even attempting to hide his excitement at their return. Joan wrapped her arms around his thick neck and buried her face in his ruff.

A big, ruddy man, Eric looked like a large, friendly dog himself. "Yeller grieves when you're gone. The others were happy as clams. Their only loyalty is to food."

Diane disappeared into the clinic with Eric and returned as Joan was getting ready to go home. "Thanks for asking me to go with you. I know you wanted to be alone."

"You're welcome, I guess, even though you nearly killed me. I'm going to start working out at home."

"Sure you are," Diane said, giving her a warm hug.

"Next time we go skiing you'll be chasing me."

At home Joan cranked up the heat, lit a fire, and turned on the television. Yeller leaned against her legs and stared raptly into her face.

"How about a little treat?" She popped a huge bowl of popcorn to share with the dog while watching *Nature* and *Masterpiece Theater*. Afterward she took the Sunday newspaper to bed to read but fell asleep before she finished the first section.

A great horned owl startled her into momentary wakefulness. She put the paper on the floor and turned on her side, ears tuned to catch the answering hoot.

The next week crawled by. Traffic was slow at the feed mill. On Wednesday she went to the Cortlands' to ride the mares. They were feisty, having been cooped up for a week, although the hired hand turned them out in the riding arena once a day.

On Friday Liz would be coming home, and that

piece of knowledge floated into Joan's consciousness off and on: at work when she was helping a customer, at the Cortlands' while she was riding the mare Liz usually rode, at Diane's as she was cleaning stalls, and Friday evening when Susie once more rode Trixie before Joan and Diane went out for fish with David.

David was saving a booth for them in a corner at Diversity. Guy was with him, still a part of his life although they were not living together.

"Where have you been? I'm three sheets to the wind, and it's all your fault."

"Diane sold Trixie tonight," Joan said.

"Does that take hours?" he asked.

"First they had to ride, then we had to talk money." Diane shrugged and smiled.

Instead of keeping the mare at Diane's the mother and daughter were taking her to a large stable. Joan would go with Diane when she delivered the mare on Sunday. One more responsibility had fallen away from Diane, one less reminder of how things had been when Tania was there, one less tie to the place.

Joan looked under the table. "Sylvester's not here, I hope."

"He's visiting with the Browns. They keep him during the day. He and Mr. Cinders are pals. Like me and Guy here." He nudged Guy, who was casing the place.

"That's us," Guy said, but Joan knew he was about to be unfaithful again.

"How was your weekend skiing?" David asked, and, when Diane smiled at Joan, said, "Something you want to share?"

"We had a good time, didn't we?" Diane said. "And don't tell them I tried to kill you."

Saturday morning at Birds of a Feather, birds jockeyed for a place at the feeders outside the windows. The thickly falling snow was mesmerizing, crystalizing on the parking lot, amassing. Joan had not heard from Liz, not even a message on her machine, and she thought maybe their brief affair was over, that perhaps Liz had given up on her, that Linda had taken her place. She still couldn't picture Linda with Lou.

The weekend skiing had made her restless, had shown her the rut that was her life. She planned to give Kathy notice before spring. She and Yeller would do some traveling when winter loosed its hold.

She picked up the book she was reading and when the door jangled stood up, holding her place with a finger. "Morning," she said before she saw that it was Liz.

Liz stood just inside the door, tanned but not rested, dressed in jeans and leather jacket. "I wanted to share Puerto Vallarta with you."

"While you and Linda basked in the sun, I went skiing with Diane," she said. "I did not sit around and feel sorry for myself."

Liz took a step toward her. "The plane was late getting in last night, too late to call you."

"Did Lou meet you at the airport?" she asked, wondering why she was so angry.

"Yes. Nice of him. He's head over heels crazy about Linda." Liz stopped to pat Yeller, who had struggled to his feet at the sound of her voice. Liz appeared uncertain, hesitant. It was in her voice, and

Joan felt herself relenting. "I shouldn't have gone. It wasn't worth it."

"Sure it was. It was a good time. Right?"

"I suppose it's stupid to ask if you want to spend the evening with me," Liz said, chewing on the inside of her mouth.

"If you don't, I'll have to ask you." The words were out of her mouth without any conscious thought.

"Your house or mine?" Liz asked, looking more puzzled than pleased.

"Mine. Six o'clock, and bring your nightie."

Summer

XIX

In August Diane turned the practice and the house over to Eric on a trial basis. She had given it a year, she told Joan. A friend from veterinary school had invited her to join her small-animal practice near Kirkland, just outside Seattle. If it worked out for her there and Eric here, Eric would buy the business and property on a contract.

Joan steeled herself against attempting to influence Diane any more. Instead she spent the second week in August helping Diane decide what to take and what to leave behind. She and Liz had taken a week off and were driving to Kirkland with Diane, spending a few days in Washington and flying back.

"You will come back some day, won't you? At least for a visit?" Joan asked as they loaded the last of the boxes and suitcases in Diane's van Friday night before their departure the next morning. Eric had bought the truck.

"Maybe when you see Washington you'll want to move there too," Diane said, promising nothing. It was like she couldn't wait to leave now that she was going, but Joan knew she wanted to be gone when the anniversary of Tania's death rolled around.

She and Liz stayed the night at Diane's, sleeping in the guest bedroom. Joan was excited about a week's vacation, a whirlwind trip across the country. Her only worry was leaving Yeller with Eric, but Eric promised to take the dog with him on calls, to keep him at his side day and night.

"Would you consider moving to Washington?" Liz asked as they lay side by side, staring at the ceiling.

"I have to see it first," she said. "Would you?"

Liz sighed. "If you were there, I would."

Saturday dawned hot, clear, and windy, and Joan thought they couldn't have a better day to travel. They pulled a rental trailer behind the van, and Joan sat in the backseat surrounded by boxes and suitcases, her hair blowing in the breeze from the open windows.

Driving west to Highway 51, they turned south to Portage where they picked up Interstate 90, which would take them across the northern tier of states. Crossing the Mississippi near La Crosse, they followed the river north a short ways before heading across Minnesota toward South Dakota. Southwestern Wisconsin was hilly and forested; southern Minnesota was prairie. The wind blew incessantly, a hot blast that tore at their hair and seared their faces, finally convincing them to close the windows and turn on the air conditioning. It was South Dakota that surprised Joan the most with its unexpected beauty. First came the prairie, and when night fell an incredible thunderstorm crashed around them, accompanied by lightning that danced everywhere. Torrential rains fell, forcing them to find shelter. The next day they crossed the Missouri, drove through the Badlands, visited the Black Hills. In Wyoming they left the interstate to drive through the Bighorns and across the state for a quick trip to Yellowstone where they saw small herds of buffalo and two moose and waited an hour for Old Faithful to weakly erupt. Mountains, waterfalls, glacial lakes, all incredibly beautiful but seen in bumper-to-bumper traffic. They drove north into Montana, picking up Interstate 90 again at Livingston and heading north and west through the Rocky Mountains and over the Continental Divide into Idaho. Then they were out of the mountains and into Spokane, Washington. All done in a few days. Crossing Washington they reached the Cascades where they made a stop at Snoqualmie Falls before turning north on U.S. 405 to Kirkland, where they somehow found the small-animal clinic and met up with Diane's friend.

They emptied the trailer and van, carrying boxes into the apartment Diane's friend had rented for her. The day was coming to an end when they brought in the last box and set it down in the small living room. Walking downtown Kirkland, they stood with the ducks and geese in a park on Lake Washington before going in search of a place to eat.

The next few days Liz and Joan drove Diane to the clinic and then went sightseeing. They found their way downtown Seattle to Pike Place Market and brought fresh salmon home for dinner; they went to the locks and took a boat tour around the harbor; they took the trolley to Pioneer Square. At night they unpacked boxes and walked around Kirkland, an upscale town on the water.

In Seattle on a sunny day, Mount Rainier rose from the horizon, whitecapped and splendid and somewhat startling, looking over the city like a benevolent god. On Saturday the three of them drove to see the mountain close-up and walked the trails through woods, past the small glacial lakes, along a thundering waterfall. Wherever they went crowds of people traveled with them. The highways were a crush of cars, speeding to some destination.

Sunday, Diane took Liz and Joan to Sea-Tac International Airport. Before they boarded the underground train that would take them to the United terminal, Diane hugged them both.

She said to Joan, who could not speak for the tears in her throat or see for those filming her eyes, "Thanks, Joanie, for all the loving care. Don't cry. Distance can never separate us."

Joan nodded and turned, stumbling toward the scanners. The train screeched to a halt, the doors slid open, and she and Liz stepped inside, where they just had time to grab a seat before the doors slammed shut and the train took off with a jerk.

They took the escalator to the terminal, found a seat at their gate, and waited to board the DC-10 that hulked at the end of the ramp.

"You'll visit, she'll visit," Liz said.

Joan sniffed and tried to smile. "I know." It was just that Diane had been a part of her life for so long that this was like tearing off an arm or a leg or a chunk of her heart.

They boarded, taking seats near the rear of the huge plane. As the interior filled with people, Joan looked out the window. The day was overcast, and Mount Rainier was lost in the clouds. Liz squeezed her hand, and Joan returned the pressure.

"It will, though," Joan said.

"What will?" Liz asked as they taxied toward takeoff.

"Distance will separate us. It always does." Could anyone maintain a close friendship from two thousand miles away?

The immense plane lifted off the ground, rose into the clouds, and turned east.

"Only if you let it," Liz said. "You'll be back, and think how much fun you'll have. You and Diane can go to Mount Saint Helens, the Olympic Peninsula, the Cascades, the wine country. I envy you. Maybe you can even drive down the Oregon coast to California. I've always wanted to do that."

"Then you'll have to come back with me," Joan said. Maybe Diane would be through grieving by then, but she doubted it. At any rate, it was time to move on.

LOOKING FOR NAIAD?

Buy our books at
www.naiadpress.com

or call our toll-free number
1-800-533-1973

or by fax (24 hours a day)
1-850-539-9731

CHANGE OF HEART by Linda Hill. 176 pp. High fashion and
love in a glamorous world.   ISBN 1-56280-238-0 $11.95

UNSTRUNG HEART by Robbi Sommers. 176 pp. Putting life
in order again.   ISBN 1-56280-239-9   11.95

BIRDS OF A FEATHER by Jackie Calhoun. 240 pp. Life begins
with love.   ISBN 1-56280-240-2   11.95

THE DRIVE by Trisha Todd. 176 pp. The star of *Claire of the
Moon* tells all!   ISBN 1-56280-237-2   11.95

BOTH SIDES by Saxon Bennett. 240 pp. A community of
women falling in and out of love.   ISBN 1-56280-236-4   11.95

WATERMARK by Karin Kallmaker. 256 pp. One burning
question . . . how to lead her back to love?   ISBN 1-56280-235-6   11.95

THE OTHER WOMAN by Ann O'Leary. 240 pp. Her roguish
way draws women like a magnet.   ISBN 1-56280-234-8   11.95

SILVER THREADS by Lyn Denison.208 pp. Finding her way
back to love . . .   ISBN 1-56280-231-3   11.95

CHIMNEY ROCK BLUES by Janet McClellan. 224 pp. 4th Tru
North mystery.   ISBN 1-56280-233-X   11.95

OMAHA'S BELL by Penny Hayes. 208 pp. Orphaned Keeley
Delaney woos the lovely Prudence Morris. ISBN 1-56280-232-1   11.95

SIXTH SENSE by Kate Calloway. 224 pp. 6th Cassidy James
mystery.   ISBN 1-56280-228-3   11.95

DAWN OF THE DANCE by Marianne K. Martin. 224 pp. A dance
with an old friend, nothing more . . . yeah!   ISBN 1-56280-229-1   11.95

WEDDING BELL BLUES by Julia Watts. 240 pp. Love, family,
and a recipe for success.   ISBN 1-56280-230-5   11.95

THOSE WHO WAIT by Peggy J. Herring. 160 pp. Two
sisters . . . in love with the same woman.   ISBN 1-56280-223-2   11.95

WHISPERS IN THE WIND by Frankie J. Jones. 192 pp. "If you don't want this," she whispered, "all you have to say is 'stop.' "
ISBN 1-56280-226-7   11.95

WHEN SOME BODY DISAPPEARS by Therese Szymanski. 192 pp. 3rd Brett Higgins mystery.   ISBN 1-56280-227-5   11.95

THE WAY LIFE SHOULD BE by Diana Braund. 240 pp. Which one will teach her the true meaning of love?   ISBN 1-56280-221-6   11.95

UNTIL THE END by Kaye Davis. 256pp. 3rd Maris Middleton mystery.   ISBN 1-56280-222-4   11.95

FIFTH WHEEL by Kate Calloway. 224 pp. 5th Cassidy James mystery.   ISBN 1-56280-218-6   11.95

JUST YESTERDAY by Linda Hill. 176 pp. Reliving all the passion of yesterday.   ISBN 1-56280-219-4   11.95

THE TOUCH OF YOUR HAND edited by Barbara Grier and Christine Cassidy. 304 pp. Erotic love stories by Naiad Press authors.   ISBN 1-56280-220-8   14.95

WINDROW GARDEN by Janet McClellan. 192 pp. They discover a passion they never dreamed possible.   ISBN 1-56280-216-X   11.95

PAST DUE by Claire McNab. 224 pp. 10th Carol Ashton mystery.   ISBN 1-56280-217-8   11.95

CHRISTABEL by Laura Adams. 224 pp. Two captive hearts and the passion that will set them free.   ISBN 1-56280-214-3   11.95

PRIVATE PASSIONS by Laura DeHart Young. 192 pp. An unforgettable new portrait of lesbian love . . .   ISBN 1-56280-215-1   11.95

BAD MOON RISING by Barbara Johnson. 208 pp. 2nd Colleen Fitzgerald mystery.   ISBN 1-56280-211-9   11.95

RIVER QUAY by Janet McClellan. 208 pp. 3rd Tru North mystery.   ISBN 1-56280-212-7   11.95

ENDLESS LOVE by Lisa Shapiro. 272 pp. To believe, once again, that love can be forever.   ISBN 1-56280-213-5   11.95

FALLEN FROM GRACE by Pat Welch. 256 pp. 6th Helen Black mystery.   ISBN 1-56280-209-7   11.95

THE NAKED EYE by Catherine Ennis. 208 pp. Her lover in the camera's eye . . .   ISBN 1-56280-210-0   11.95

OVER THE LINE by Tracey Richardson. 176 pp. 2nd Stevie Houston mystery.   ISBN 1-56280-202-X   11.95

JULIA'S SONG by Ann O'Leary. 208 pp. Strangely disturbing . . . strangely exciting.   ISBN 1-56280-197-X   11.95

LOVE IN THE BALANCE by Marianne K. Martin. 256 pp. Weighing the costs of love . . .   ISBN 1-56280-199-6   11.95

PIECE OF MY HEART by Julia Watts. 208 pp. All the stuff that dreams are made of —   ISBN 1-56280-206-2   11.95

MAKING UP FOR LOST TIME by Karin Kallmaker. 240 pp.
Nobody does it better . . .   ISBN 1-56280-196-1   11.95

GOLD FEVER by Lyn Denison. 224 pp. By author of *Dream
Lover.*   ISBN 1-56280-201-1   11.95

WHEN THE DEAD SPEAK by Therese Szymanski. 224 pp. 2nd
Brett Higgins mystery.   ISBN 1-56280-198-8   11.95

FOURTH DOWN by Kate Calloway. 240 pp. 4th Cassidy James
mystery.   ISBN 1-56280-205-4   11.95

A MOMENT'S INDISCRETION by Peggy J. Herring. 176 pp.
There's a fine line between love and lust . . .   ISBN 1-56280-194-5   11.95

CITY LIGHTS/COUNTRY CANDLES by Penny Hayes. 208 pp.
About the women she has known . . .   ISBN 1-56280-195-3   11.95

POSSESSIONS by Kaye Davis. 240 pp. 2nd Maris Middleton
mystery.   ISBN 1-56280-192-9   11.95

A QUESTION OF LOVE by Saxon Bennett. 208 pp. Every
woman is granted one great love.   ISBN 1-56280-205-4   11.95

RHYTHM TIDE by Frankie J. Jones. 160 pp.   . . . to desire
passionately and be passionately desired.   ISBN 1-56280-189-9   11.95

PENN VALLEY PHOENIX by Janet McClellan. 208 pp. 2nd
Tru North Mystery.   ISBN 1-56280-200-3   11.95

BY RESERVATION ONLY by Jackie Calhoun. 240 pp. A
chance for true happiness.   ISBN 1-56280-191-0   11.95

OLD BLACK MAGIC by Jaye Maiman. 272 pp. 9th Robin
Miller mystery.   ISBN 1-56280-175-9   11.95

LEGACY OF LOVE by Marianne K. Martin. 240 pp. Women
will do anything for her . . .   ISBN 1-56280-184-8   11.95

LETTING GO by Ann O'Leary. 160 pp. Laura, at 39, in love
with 23-year-old Kate.   ISBN 1-56280-183-X   11.95

LADY BE GOOD edited by Barbara Grier and Christine Cassidy.
288 pp. Erotic stories by Naiad Press authors.   ISBN 1-56280-180-5   14.95

CHAIN LETTER by Claire McNab. 288 pp. 9th Carol Ashton
mystery.   ISBN 1-56280-181-3   11.95

NIGHT VISION by Laura Adams. 256 pp. Erotic fantasy romance
by "famous" author.   ISBN 1-56280-182-1   11.95

SEA TO SHINING SEA by Lisa Shapiro. 256 pp. Unable to resist
the raging passion . . .   ISBN 1-56280-177-5   11.95

THIRD DEGREE by Kate Calloway. 224 pp. 3rd Cassidy James
mystery.   ISBN 1-56280-185-6   11.95

WHEN THE DANCING STOPS by Therese Szymanski. 272 pp.
1st Brett Higgins mystery.   ISBN 1-56280-186-4   11.95

PHASES OF THE MOON by Julia Watts. 192 pp. . . . . . hungry
for everything life has to offer.   ISBN 1-56280-176-7   11.95

BABY IT'S COLD by Jaye Maiman. 256 pp. 5th Robin Miller
mystery.   ISBN 1-56280-156-2   10.95

CLASS REUNION by Linda Hill. 176 pp. The girl from her
past . . .   ISBN 1-56280-178-3   11.95

DREAM LOVER by Lyn Denison. 224 pp. A soft, sensuous,
romantic fantasy.   ISBN 1-56280-173-1   11.95

FORTY LOVE by Diana Simmonds. 288 pp. Joyous, heart-
warming romance.   ISBN 1-56280-171-6   11.95

IN THE MOOD by Robbi Sommers. 160 pp. The queen of
erotic tension!   ISBN 1-56280-172-4   11.95

SWIMMING CAT COVE by Lauren Douglas. 192 pp. 2nd
Allison O'Neil Mystery.   ISBN 1-56280-168-6   11.95

THE LOVING LESBIAN by Claire McNab and Sharon Gedan.
240 pp. Explore the experiences that make lesbian love unique.
                                             ISBN 1-56280-169-4   14.95

COURTED by Celia Cohen. 160 pp. Sparkling romantic
encounter.   ISBN 1-56280-166-X   11.95

SEASONS OF THE HEART by Jackie Calhoun. 240 pp. Romance
through the years.   ISBN 1-56280-167-8   11.95

K. C. BOMBER by Janet McClellan. 208 pp. 1st Tru North
mystery.   ISBN 1-56280-157-0   11.95

LAST RITES by Tracey Richardson. 192 pp. 1st Stevie Houston
mystery.   ISBN 1-56280-164-3   11.95

EMBRACE IN MOTION by Karin Kallmaker. 256 pp. A whirlwind
love affair.   ISBN 1-56280-165-1   11.95

HOT CHECK by Peggy J. Herring. 192 pp. Will workaholic Alice
fall for guitarist Ricky?   ISBN 1-56280-163-5   11.95

OLD TIES by Saxon Bennett. 176 pp. Can Cleo surrender to a
passionate new love?   ISBN 1-56280-159-7   11.95

LOVE ON THE LINE by Laura DeHart Young. 176 pp. Will Stef
win Kay's heart?   ISBN 1-56280-162-7   11.95

DEVIL'S LEG CROSSING by Kaye Davis. 192 pp. 1st Maris
Middleton mystery.   ISBN 1-56280-158-9   11.95

COSTA BRAVA by Marta Balletbo Coll. 144 pp. Read the book,
see the movie!   ISBN 1-56280-153-8   11.95

MEETING MAGDALENE & OTHER STORIES by
Marilyn Freeman. 144 pp. Read the book, see the movie!
                                             ISBN 1-56280-170-8   11.95

SECOND FIDDLE by Kate 208 pp. 2nd P.I. Cassidy James
mystery.   ISBN 1-56280-169-6   11.95

LAUREL by Isabel Miller. 128 pp. By the author of the beloved
Patience and Sarah.   ISBN 1-56280-146-5   10.95

LOVE OR MONEY by Jackie Calhoun. 240 pp. The romance of
real life.   ISBN 1-56280-147-3   10.95

SMOKE AND MIRRORS by Pat Welch. 224 pp. 5th Helen Black
Mystery.   ISBN 1-56280-143-0   10.95

DANCING IN THE DARK edited by Barbara Grier & Christine
Cassidy. 272 pp. Erotic love stories by Naiad Press authors.
                                              ISBN 1-56280-144-9   14.95

TIME AND TIME AGAIN by Catherine Ennis. 176 pp. Passionate
love affair.   ISBN 1-56280-145-7   10.95

PAXTON COURT by Diane Salvatore. 256 pp. Erotic and wickedly
funny contemporary tale about the business of learning to live
together.   ISBN 1-56280-114-7   10.95

INNER CIRCLE by Claire McNab. 208 pp. 8th Carol Ashton
Mystery.   ISBN 1-56280-135-X   11.95

LESBIAN SEX: AN ORAL HISTORY by Susan Johnson.
240 pp. Need we say more?   ISBN 1-56280-142-2   14.95

WILD THINGS by Karin Kallmaker. 240 pp. By the undisputed
mistress of lesbian romance.   ISBN 1-56280-139-2   11.95

THE GIRL NEXT DOOR by Mindy Kaplan. 208 pp. Just what
you d expect.   ISBN 1-56280-140-6   11.95

NOW AND THEN by Penny Hayes. 240 pp. Romance on the
westward journey.   ISBN 1-56280-121-X   11.95

HEART ON FIRE by Diana Simmonds. 176 pp. The romantic and
erotic rival of *Curious Wine*.   ISBN 1-56280-152-X   11.95

DEATH AT LAVENDER BAY by Lauren Wright Douglas. 208 pp.
1st Allison O'Neil Mystery.   ISBN 1-56280-085-X   11.95

YES I SAID YES I WILL by Judith McDaniel. 272 pp. Hot
romance by famous author.   ISBN 1-56280-138-4   11.95

FORBIDDEN FIRES by Margaret C. Anderson. Edited by Mathilda
Hills. 176 pp. Famous author's "unpublished" Lesbian romance.
                                              ISBN 1-56280-123-6   21.95

SIDE TRACKS by Teresa Stores. 160 pp. Gender-bending
Lesbians on the road.   ISBN 1-56280-122-8   10.95

WILDWOOD FLOWERS by Julia Watts. 208 pp. Hilarious and
heart-warming tale of true love.   ISBN 1-56280-127-9   10.95

NEVER SAY NEVER by Linda Hill. 224 pp. Rule #1: Never get
involved with . . .   ISBN 1-56280-126-0   11.95

THE WISH LIST by Saxon Bennett. 192 pp. Romance through
the years.   ISBN 1-56280-125-2   10.95

OUT OF THE NIGHT by Kris Bruyer. 192 pp. Spine-tingling
thriller.   ISBN 1-56280-120-1   10.95

LOVE'S HARVEST by Peggy J. Herring. 176 pp. by the author of
Once More With Feeling.   ISBN 1-56280-117-1   10.95

FAMILY SECRETS by Laura DeHart Young. 208 pp. Enthralling
romance and suspense.   ISBN 1-56280-119-8   10.95

INLAND PASSAGE by Jane Rule. 288 pp. Tales exploring conven-
tional & unconventional relationships.   ISBN 0-930044-56-8   10.95

DOUBLE BLUFF by Claire McNab. 208 pp. 7th Carol Ashton
Mystery.   ISBN 1-56280-096-5   10.95

BAR GIRLS by Lauran Hoffman. 176 pp. See the movie, read
the book!   ISBN 1-56280-115-5   10.95

THE FIRST TIME EVER edited by Barbara Grier & Christine
Cassidy. 272 pp. Love stories by Naiad Press authors.
                                             ISBN 1-56280-086-8   14.95

MISS PETTIBONE AND MISS McGRAW by Brenda Weathers.
208 pp. A charming ghostly love story.   ISBN 1-56280-151-1   10.95

CHANGES by Jackie Calhoun. 208 pp. Involved romance and
relationships.   ISBN 1-56280-083-3   10.95

FAIR PLAY by Rose Beecham. 256 pp. An Amanda Valentine
Mystery.   ISBN 1-56280-081-7   10.95

PAYBACK by Celia Cohen. 176 pp. A gripping thriller of romance,
revenge and betrayal.   ISBN 1-56280-084-1   10.95

THE BEACH AFFAIR by Barbara Johnson. 224 pp. Sizzling
summer romance/mystery/intrigue.   ISBN 1-56280-090-6   10.95

GETTING THERE by Robbi Sommers. 192 pp. Nobody does it
like Robbi!   ISBN 1-56280-099-X   10.95

FINAL CUT by Lisa Haddock. 208 pp. 2nd Carmen Ramirez
Mystery.   ISBN 1-56280-088-4   10.95

FLASHPOINT by Katherine V. Forrest. 256 pp. A Lesbian
blockbuster!   ISBN 1-56280-079-5   10.95

CLAIRE OF THE MOON by Nicole Conn. Audio Book —
Read by Marianne Hyatt.   ISBN 1-56280-113-9   16.95

FOR LOVE AND FOR LIFE: INTIMATE PORTRAITS OF
LESBIAN COUPLES by Susan Johnson. 224 pp.
                                             ISBN 1-56280-091-4   14.95

DEVOTION by Mindy Kaplan. 192 pp. See the movie — read
the book!   ISBN 1-56280-093-0   10.95

SOMEONE TO WATCH by Jaye Maiman. 272 pp. 4th Robin
Miller Mystery.   ISBN 1-56280-095-7   10.95

GREENER THAN GRASS by Jennifer Fulton. 208 pp. A young
woman — a stranger in her bed.   ISBN 1-56280-092-2   10.95

TRAVELS WITH DIANA HUNTER by Regine Sands. Erotic
lesbian romp. Audio Book (2 cassettes)   ISBN 1-56280-107-4   16.95

CABIN FEVER by Carol Schmidt. 256 pp. Sizzling suspense
and passion. ISBN 1-56280-089-1 10.95

THERE WILL BE NO GOODBYES by Laura DeHart Young. 192
pp. Romantic love, strength, and friendship. ISBN 1-56280-103-1 10.95

FAULTLINE by Sheila Ortiz Taylor. 144 pp. Joyous comic
lesbian novel. ISBN 1-56280-108-2 9.95

OPEN HOUSE by Pat Welch. 176 pp. 4th Helen Black Mystery.
ISBN 1-56280-102-3 10.95

ONCE MORE WITH FEELING by Peggy J. Herring. 240 pp.
Lighthearted, loving romantic adventure. ISBN 1-56280-089-2 11.95

WHISPERS by Kris Bruyer. 176 pp. Romantic ghost story.
ISBN 1-56280-082-5 10.95

NIGHT SONGS by Penny Mickelbury. 224 pp. 2nd Gianna
Maglione Mystery. ISBN 1-56280-097-3 10.95

GETTING TO THE POINT by Teresa Stores. 256 pp. Classic
southern Lesbian novel. ISBN 1-56280-100-7 10.95

PAINTED MOON by Karin Kallmaker. 224 pp. Delicious
Kallmaker romance. ISBN 1-56280-075-2 11.95

THE MYSTERIOUS NAIAD edited by Katherine V. Forrest &
Barbara Grier. 320 pp. Love stories by Naiad Press authors.
ISBN 1-56280-074-4 14.95

DAUGHTERS OF A CORAL DAWN by Katherine V. Forrest.
240 pp. Tenth Anniversay Edition. ISBN 1-56280-104-X 11.95

BODY GUARD by Claire McNab. 208 pp. 6th Carol Ashton
Mystery. ISBN 1-56280-073-6 11.95

CACTUS LOVE by Lee Lynch. 192 pp. Stories by the beloved
storyteller. ISBN 1-56280-071-X 9.95

SECOND GUESS by Rose Beecham. 216 pp. An Amanda
Valentine Mystery. ISBN 1-56280-069-8 9.95

A RAGE OF MAIDENS by Lauren Wright Douglas. 240 pp.
6th Caitlin Reece Mystery. ISBN 1-56280-068-X 10.95

TRIPLE EXPOSURE by Jackie Calhoun. 224 pp. Romantic
drama involving many characters. ISBN 1-56280-067-1 10.95

PERSONAL ADS by Robbi Sommers. 176 pp. Sizzling short
stories. ISBN 1-56280-059-0 11.95

CROSSWORDS by Penny Sumner. 256 pp. 2nd Victoria Cross
Mystery. ISBN 1-56280-064-7 9.95

SWEET CHERRY WINE by Carol Schmidt. 224 pp. A novel of
suspense. ISBN 1-56280-063-9 9.95

CERTAIN SMILES by Dorothy Tell. 160 pp. Erotic short stories.
ISBN 1-56280-066-3 9.95

EDITED OUT by Lisa Haddock. 224 pp. 1st Carmen Ramirez
Mystery.   ISBN 1-56280-077-9   9.95

SMOKEY O by Celia Cohen. 176 pp. Relationships on the
playing field.   ISBN 1-56280-057-4   9.95

KATHLEEN O'DONALD by Penny Hayes. 256 pp. Rose and
Kathleen find each other and employment in 1909 NYC.
                                      ISBN 1-56280-070-1   9.95

STAYING HOME by Elisabeth Nonas. 256 pp. Molly and Alix
want a baby . . . or do they?   ISBN 1-56280-076-0   10.95

TRUE LOVE by Jennifer Fulton. 240 pp. Six lesbians searching
for love in all the "right" places. ISBN 1-56280-035-3   11.95

KEEPING SECRETS by Penny Mickelbury. 208 pp. 1st Gianna
Maglione Mystery.   ISBN 1-56280-052-3   9.95

THE ROMANTIC NAIAD edited by Katherine V. Forrest &
Barbara Grier. 336 pp. Love stories by Naiad Press authors.
                                      ISBN 1-56280-054-X   14.95

UNDER MY SKIN by Jaye Maiman. 336 pp. 3rd Robin Miller
Mystery.   ISBN 1-56280-049-3.   11.95

CAR POOL by Karin Kallmaker. 272pp. Lesbians on wheels
and then some!   ISBN 1-56280-048-5   11.95

NOT TELLING MOTHER: STORIES FROM A LIFE by Diane
Salvatore. 176 pp. Her 3rd novel.   ISBN 1-56280-044-2   9.95

GOBLIN MARKET by Lauren Wright Douglas. 240pp. 5th Caitlin
Reece Mystery.   ISBN 1-56280-047-7   10.95

FRIENDS AND LOVERS by Jackie Calhoun. 224 pp. Mid-
western Lesbian lives and loves.   ISBN 1-56280-041-8   11.95

BEHIND CLOSED DOORS by Robbi Sommers. 192 pp. Hot,
erotic short stories.   ISBN 1-56280-039-6   11.95

CLAIRE OF THE MOON by Nicole Conn. 192 pp. See the
movie — read the book!   ISBN 1-56280-038-8   11.95

SILENT HEART by Claire McNab. 192 pp. Exotic Lesbian
romance.   ISBN 1-56280-036-1   11.95

THE SPY IN QUESTION by Amanda Kyle Williams. 256 pp.
A Madison McGuire Mystery.   ISBN 1-56280-037-X   9.95

SAVING GRACE by Jennifer Fulton. 240 pp. Adventure and
romantic entanglement.   ISBN 1-56280-051-5   11.95

CURIOUS WINE by Katherine V. Forrest. 176 pp. Tenth Anniversary Edition. The most popular contemporary Lesbian love story.
                                      ISBN 1-56280-053-1   11.95
    Audio Book (2 cassettes)   ISBN 1-56280-105-8   16.95

CHAUTAUQUA by Catherine Ennis. 192 pp. Exciting, romantic
adventure.   ISBN 1-56280-032-9   9.95

A PROPER BURIAL by Pat Welch. 192 pp. 3rd Helen Black
Mystery. ISBN 1-56280-033-7   9.95

SILVERLAKE HEAT: A Novel of Suspense by Carol Schmidt.
240 pp. Rhonda is as hot as Laney's dreams. ISBN 1-56280-031-0   9.95

LOVE, ZENA BETH by Diane Salvatore. 224 pp. The most talked
about lesbian novel of the nineties! ISBN 1-56280-030-2   10.95

A DOORYARD FULL OF FLOWERS by Isabel Miller. 160 pp.
Stories incl. 2 sequels to *Patience and Sarah.* ISBN 1-56280-029-9   9.95

MURDER BY TRADITION by Katherine V. Forrest. 288 pp. 4th
Kate Delafield Mystery. ISBN 1-56280-002-7   11.95

THE EROTIC NAIAD edited by Katherine V. Forrest & Barbara
Grier. 224 pp. Love stories by Naiad Press authors.
ISBN 1-56280-026-4   14.95

DEAD CERTAIN by Claire McNab. 224 pp. 5th Carol Ashton
Mystery. ISBN 1-56280-027-2   9.95

CRAZY FOR LOVING by Jaye Maiman. 320 pp. 2nd Robin Miller
Mystery. ISBN 1-56280-025-6   11.95

UNCERTAIN COMPANIONS by Robbi Sommers. 204 pp.
Steamy, erotic novel. ISBN 1-56280-017-5   11.95

A TIGER'S HEART by Lauren W. Douglas. 240 pp. 4th Caitlin
Reece Mystery. ISBN 1-56280-018-3   9.95

PAPERBACK ROMANCE by Karin Kallmaker. 256 pp. A
delicious romance. ISBN 1-56280-019-1   10.95

THE LAVENDER HOUSE MURDER by Nikki Baker. 224 pp.
2nd Virginia Kelly Mystery. ISBN 1-56280-012-4   9.95

PASSION BAY by Jennifer Fulton. 224 pp. Passionate romance,
virgin beaches, tropical skies. ISBN 1-56280-028-0   10.95

STICKS AND STONES by Jackie Calhoun. 208 pp. Contemporary
lesbian lives and loves. ISBN 1-56280-020-5   9.95
Audio Book (2 cassettes) ISBN 1-56280-106-6   16.95

UNDER THE SOUTHERN CROSS by Claire McNab. 192 pp.
Romantic nights Down Under. ISBN 1-56280-011-6   11.95

GRASSY FLATS by Penny Hayes. 256 pp. Lesbian romance in
the '30s. ISBN 1-56280-010-8   9.95

THE END OF APRIL by Penny Sumner. 240 pp. 1st Victoria
Cross Mystery. ISBN 1-56280-007-8   8.95

KISS AND TELL by Robbi Sommers. 192 pp. Scorching stories
by the author of *Pleasures.* ISBN 1-56280-005-1   11.95

STILL WATERS by Pat Welch. 208 pp. 2nd Helen Black Mystery.
ISBN 0-941483-97-5   9.95

TO LOVE AGAIN by Evelyn Kennedy. 208 pp. Wildly romantic
love story. ISBN 0-941483-85-1   11.95

IN THE GAME by Nikki Baker. 192 pp. 1st Virginia Kelly
Mystery.   ISBN 1-56280-004-3   9.95

STRANDED by Camarin Grae. 320 pp. Entertaining, riveting
adventure.   ISBN 0-941483-99-1   9.95

THE DAUGHTERS OF ARTEMIS by Lauren Wright Douglas.
240 pp. 3rd Caitlin Reece Mystery.   ISBN 0-941483-95-9   9.95

CLEARWATER by Catherine Ennis. 176 pp. Romantic secrets
of a small Louisiana town.   ISBN 0-941483-65-7   8.95

THE HALLELUJAH MURDERS by Dorothy Tell. 176 pp. 2nd
Poppy Dillworth Mystery.   ISBN 0-941483-88-6   8.95

BENEDICTION by Diane Salvatore. 272 pp. Striking, contemporary romantic novel.   ISBN 0-941483-90-8   11.95

COP OUT by Claire McNab. 208 pp. 4th Carol Ashton Mystery.
                                            ISBN 0-941483-84-3   10.95

THE BEVERLY MALIBU by Katherine V. Forrest. 288 pp. 3rd
Kate Delafield Mystery.   ISBN 0-941483-48-7   11.95

THE PROVIDENCE FILE by Amanda Kyle Williams. 256 pp.
A Madison McGuire Mystery.   ISBN 0-941483-92-4   8.95

I LEFT MY HEART by Jaye Maiman. 320 pp. 1st Robin Miller
Mystery.   ISBN 0-941483-72-X   11.95

THE PRICE OF SALT by Patricia Highsmith (writing as Claire
Morgan). 288 pp. Classic lesbian novel, first issued in 1952 . . .
acknowledged by its author under her own, very famous, name.
                                            ISBN 1-56280-003-5   11.95

SIDE BY SIDE by Isabel Miller. 256 pp. From beloved author of
Patience and Sarah.   ISBN 0-941483-77-0   10.95

STAYING POWER: LONG TERM LESBIAN COUPLES by
Susan E. Johnson. 352 pp. Joys of coupledom. ISBN 0-941-483-75-4   14.95

SLICK by Camarin Grae. 304 pp. Exotic, erotic adventure.
                                            ISBN 0-941483-74-6   9.95

NINTH LIFE by Lauren Wright Douglas. 256 pp. 2nd Caitlin
Reece Mystery.   ISBN 0-941483-50-9   9.95

PLAYERS by Robbi Sommers. 192 pp. Sizzling, erotic novel.
                                            ISBN 0-941483-73-8   9.95

MURDER AT RED ROOK RANCH by Dorothy Tell. 224 pp.
1st Poppy Dillworth Mystery.   ISBN 0-941483-80-0   8.95

A ROOM FULL OF WOMEN by Elisabeth Nonas. 256 pp.
Contemporary Lesbian lives.   ISBN 0-941483-69-X   9.95

THEME FOR DIVERSE INSTRUMENTS by Jane Rule. 208 pp.
Powerful romantic lesbian stories.   ISBN 0-941483-63-0   8.95

CLUB 12 by Amanda Kyle Williams. 288 pp. Espionage thriller
featuring a lesbian agent!   ISBN 0-941483-64-9   9.95

DEATH DOWN UNDER by Claire McNab. 240 pp. 3rd Carol
Ashton Mystery. ISBN 0-941483-39-8   11.95

MONTANA FEATHERS by Penny Hayes. 256 pp. Vivian and
Elizabeth find love in frontier Montana. ISBN 0-941483-61-4   9.95

THERE'S SOMETHING I'VE BEEN MEANING TO TELL YOU
Ed. by Loralee MacPike. 288 pp. Gay men and lesbians coming out
to their children. ISBN 0-941483-44-4   9.95

LIFTING BELLY by Gertrude Stein. Ed. by Rebecca Mark. 104 pp.
Erotic poetry. ISBN 0-941483-51-7   10.95

AFTER THE FIRE by Jane Rule. 256 pp. Warm, human novel by
this incomparable author. ISBN 0-941483-45-2   8.95

PLEASURES by Robbi Sommers. 204 pp. Unprecedented
eroticism. ISBN 0-941483-49-5   11.95

EDGEWISE by Camarin Grae. 372 pp. Spellbinding
adventure. ISBN 0-941483-19-3   9.95

FATAL REUNION by Claire McNab. 224 pp. 2nd Carol Ashton
Mystery. ISBN 0-941483-40-1   11.95

IN EVERY PORT by Karin Kallmaker. 228 pp. Jessica's sexy,
adventuresome travels. ISBN 0-941483-37-7   11.95

OF LOVE AND GLORY by Evelyn Kennedy. 192 pp. Exciting
WWII romance. ISBN 0-941483-32-0   10.95

CLICKING STONES by Nancy Tyler Glenn. 288 pp. Love
transcending time. ISBN 0-941483-31-2   9.95

SOUTH OF THE LINE by Catherine Ennis. 216 pp. Civil War
adventure. ISBN 0-941483-29-0   8.95

WOMAN PLUS WOMAN by Dolores Klaich. 300 pp. Supurb
Lesbian overview. ISBN 0-941483-28-2   9.95

THE FINER GRAIN by Denise Ohio. 216 pp. Brilliant young
college lesbian novel. ISBN 0-941483-11-8   8.95

LESSONS IN MURDER by Claire McNab. 216 pp. 1st Carol Ashton
Mystery. ISBN 0-941483-14-2   11.95

YELLOWTHROAT by Penny Hayes. 240 pp. Margarita, bandit,
kidnaps Julia. ISBN 0-941483-10-X   8.95

SAPPHISTRY: THE BOOK OF LESBIAN SEXUALITY by
Pat Califia. 3d edition, revised. 208 pp. ISBN 0-941483-24-X   12.95

CHERISHED LOVE by Evelyn Kennedy. 192 pp. Erotic Lesbian
love story. ISBN 0-941483-08-8   11.95

THE SECRET IN THE BIRD by Camarin Grae. 312 pp. Striking,
psychological suspense novel. ISBN 0-941483-05-3   8.95

TO THE LIGHTNING by Catherine Ennis. 208 pp. Romantic
Lesbian `Robinson Crusoe adventure. ISBN 0-941483-06-1   8.95

DREAMS AND SWORDS by Katherine V. Forrest. 192 pp.
Romantic, erotic, imaginative stories.　　　ISBN 0-941483-03-7　11.95

MEMORY BOARD by Jane Rule. 336 pp. Memorable novel
about an aging Lesbian couple.　　　ISBN 0-941483-02-9　12.95

THE ALWAYS ANONYMOUS BEAST by Lauren Wright Douglas.
224 pp. 1st Caitlin Reece Mystery.　　　ISBN 0-941483-04-5　8.95

MURDER AT THE NIGHTWOOD BAR by Katherine V. Forrest.
240 pp. 2nd Kate Delafield Mystery.　　　ISBN 0-930044-92-4　11.95

WINGED DANCER by Camarin Grae. 228 pp. Erotic Lesbian
adventure story.　　　ISBN 0-930044-88-6　8.95

PAZ by Camarin Grae. 336 pp. Romantic Lesbian adventurer
with the power to change the world.　　　ISBN 0-930044-89-4　8.95

SOUL SNATCHER by Camarin Grae. 224 pp. A puzzle, an
adventure, a mystery — Lesbian romance.　ISBN 0-930044-90-8　8.95

THE LOVE OF GOOD WOMEN by Isabel Miller. 224 pp.
Long-awaited new novel by the author of the beloved *Patience
and Sarah.*　　　ISBN 0-930044-81-9　8.95

THE LONG TRAIL by Penny Hayes. 248 pp. Vivid adventures
of two women in love in the old west.　ISBN 0-930044-76-2　8.95

AN EMERGENCE OF GREEN by Katherine V. Forrest. 288
pp. Powerful novel of sexual discovery.　ISBN 0-930044-69-X　11.95

DESERT OF THE HEART by Jane Rule. 224 pp. A classic;
basis for the movie *Desert Hearts.*　　ISBN 0-930044-73-8　11.95

SEX VARIANT WOMEN IN LITERATURE by Jeannette
Howard Foster. 448 pp. Literary history.　ISBN 0-930044-65-7　8.95

A HOT-EYED MODERATE by Jane Rule. 252 pp. Hard-hitting
essays on gay life; writing; art.　　　ISBN 0-930044-57-6　7.95

AMATEUR CITY by Katherine V. Forrest. 224 pp. 1st Kate
Delafield Mystery.　　　ISBN 0-930044-55-X　10.95

THE SOPHIE HOROWITZ STORY by Sarah Schulman. 176 pp.
Engaging novel of madcap intrigue.　　ISBN 0-930044-54-1　7.95

THE YOUNG IN ONE ANOTHER'S ARMS by Jane Rule.
224 pp. Classic Jane Rule.　　　ISBN 0-930044-53-3　9.95

AGAINST THE SEASON by Jane Rule. 224 pp. Luminous,
complex novel of interrelationships.　　ISBN 0-930044-48-7　8.95

These are just a few of the many Naiad Press titles — we are the oldest and
largest lesbian/feminist publishing company in the world. We also offer an
enormous selection of lesbian video products. Please request a complete
catalog. We offer personal service; we encourage and welcome direct mail
orders from individuals who have limited access to bookstores carrying our
publications.